DELTA 23

HARRY F. BUNN

First published in 2024

All rights reserved. No part of this publication may be reproduced, stored in, or included in a retrievable system or transmitted in any form, or by any means, without the written permission of the author.

Copyright © 2024 by Harry F. Bunn

DISCLAIMER

Delta23 is a work of fiction set in 2091. The characters are fictitious and conjured up by the author's mind. The author is also responsible for worldbuilding— his scenario for the technological and societal aspects of that future time.

Cover image of asteroid: Courtesy of NASA
ISBN 9798327220836

To my wife, Jackie, for her support and love over the years.

Thanks too, to Kelly and Michael for pre-reading the book and offering their great insights.

Table of Contents

Chapter One 2

Chapter Two 16

Chapter Three 33

Chapter Four 51

Chapter Five 72

Chapter Six 88

Chapter Seven 109

Chapter Eight 129

Chapter Nine 140

Chapter Ten 153

Chapter Eleven 171

Chapter Twelve 188

Chapter Thirteen 203

Chapter Fourteen 227

Chapter Fifteen 243

Chapter Sixteen 258

Chapter Seventeen 280

Chapter Eighteen 299

Chapter Nineteen 308

A Note from the Author - Worldbuilding 317

About the Author: 322

Prologue

Only a few people know that, in 2091, Earthlings faced a threat that could have destroyed the human race. The world government and corporations have kept the matter secret, but I know the truth of what transpired because I was personally involved. This is my story.

The episode lasted less than six Earth months and at the end of that time, my adventure could have ended with me being almost anywhere in the Solar System.

Why don't you guess where that was? I'll give you some possibilities to choose from.

1. In solitary confinement at a penal colony on Saturn.

2. On an island in the Caribbean.

3. In a spacecraft nearly three hundred million kilometers from Earth… being pursued by Space Marshals.

4. On an unpopulated piece of rock five hundred million kilometers from Earth. An asteroid called Delta23.

No peeking to the end of the book!

Hut Mur
Space Tractor Captain
2092

Chapter One

My name is Hut Mur, and my story starts in January 2091 as I approached a fuel station on Mars.

My forward screens revealed a structure that had seen better days and I was unhappy with what I saw. The docking gantries that would secure my craft through refueling looked old and heavily corroded. The facility, known as the M1 depot, was the oldest fueling point outside Earth, though I had not visited it before.

When the initial settlement was built in 2049, it was constructed on the planet's surface. The main colony was later moved to a superior site on the far side of the planet, but the leaders decided to leave the fuel depot where it was. The only attraction of M1 was that fuel additives were cheaper than in other depots in the zone. I was low on propellant additives, and my funds were also low, and M1 seemed like a good option.

My spacecraft was twenty years old and categorized as a space tractor, but it was my pride and joy. I regarded it as spacious and equipped to make travel as comfortable as possible for trips across the Solar System that could last months. Owing to its age, it did not have all the latest features, but it performed well, and my monthly loan payments were reasonable.

The heart of my ship was the Control Center, which was compact with two forward seats and, behind them, two others offering observation positions. All the seats faced a collection of dynamic screens that could be configured to show various views from the vessel, as well as metrics that indicated our position, speed, propellant additive levels, and all the other data I needed to monitor operations. My seat was old but comfortable; it had stayed the same since the ship was constructed. The right chair was newer and had been designed for my second-in-command. It was lower to the deck but more than twice the width of mine.

Adjoining the Control Center was a sizable lounge with a single three-seater couch and two armchairs. At the end of the lounge was a dining and food preparation area. Three numbered doors led to sleep cabins, that the former owner had called staterooms when he sold me the vessel. They were comfortable but by no means staterooms. My number two occupied the largest cabin, normally reserved for the captain, and I used one of the other two. Each had an en suite bathroom and there was a restroom between the lounge and the Control Center.

The living quarters, however, constituted a small part of the tractor. The twin ion thruster engines constituted the most significant area by far. Access to these and other areas in the spacecraft was from the Control Center.

I glanced at a wall clock which indicated that the time was 11:00 AM. There are no days and nights when traveling in space, so captains set up their vessels to emulate Earth's time zones, sleeping to a pattern similar to Earth with meals at regular Earth times. I calibrated my ship to mirror Eastern Time reflecting my hometown in the New York part of the States of North America and this setting programmed the lighting, clocks, and calendar functions.

Although my spacecraft was pre-owned and old, it had served me well for the five years since I purchased it, and it was reliable for transporting quantities of ore and metals from one heavenly body to another. However, the business was intermittent, and I needed to make payments for the loan on my vessel every Earth month, and lately, that had become an issue. But, I was feeling happier than I had been a week before as I had just landed a significant contract and the fee for this would allow me to satisfy my lender for several months. Unfortunately, I would not receive the first payment for about sixty days and a loan installment was due in just three weeks.

The job was straightforward. I would fly to Enceladus, one of Saturn's moons which holds more water, albeit frozen, than in all of Earth's oceans, and here I would collect ten containers of ice – four and a quarter million liters - and transport most of it to a resort complex on

Ganymede. My journey would then bring me back to Mars to deliver the remainder to the expanded Earth settlement there. Although Mars had a water supply, it was of poor quality compared with that of the Saturn moon.

However, before embarking on this trip, I needed to refuel my tractor, and looking out at the M1 station, I shook my head.

Turning my attention to an image from a rear-facing camera, I looked out at my ten cargo trailers. Each was one hundred meters long and hung in a magnetically attached string to my vessel. While I refueled, I would leave the cargo pods in space, so I spoke. "Operations Command."

A blue light illuminated, indicating that the system had picked up my wake-up command. "Disconnect pods."

My ship's major functions are activated by a series of voice-controlled AI bots and, when I purchased the craft, I programmed these to speak in female voices with different accents for each function. One with a French accent, one British, one Mexican, and so on. This made it easier to determine to which I was talking. I watched as the trailers separated and the system spoke to me with a British accent. "Disconnected, Hut."

With the pods separated, I was ready to activate the procedure that would take me to the refueling dock, but after looking at the state of decay on the berthing equipment before me, I thought again.

Skrog, my number two, came onto the control deck and squinted out of his three left eyes at the scene unfolding below.

"Look pretty bad place, Cap." His translation system, Martian to English, worked well enough but not perfectly.

"I agree. It's seen better times."

"You hesitation, Cap."

"You're right. I am hesitating, Skrog."

He wore a rubber-like pressure suit like mine. The suits were short and covered the trunk from the neck but not the legs or arms. They were cumbersome but more comfortable than the full-body suits of years gone by. Skrog's suit was similar, but the shape was significantly different, being wrapped around the four-foot, three-hundred-pound native whose ancestors had been from some planet beyond the Solar System but were referred to by humans as Martians.

Skrog's movement was more sliding than walking, as, to move, he relied on the twenty or so toes, that he had on each of his two feet. He was an excellent second officer and knew more about the various ports of call we visited than I did. With just a few exceptions, he kept us out of trouble, but I thought back to one of those incidents and smiled. How did we ever avoid getting ourselves killed on Uranus2?

The communications system broke through my thoughts. Someone in the planet commander's office had called me on the local holo-channel.

Despite its age, my ship had an up-to-date, commercial-grade holo-call technology that created a high-definition holographic image of each caller.

I stepped into the hologram and, virtually, joined a man from the planet, a human who was, perhaps, five foot eight and dressed in standard trucker overalls. His clothing needed repair, and it gave me the impression that it had not been cleaned lately.

He greeted me. "Welcome to Fueling Station M1."

He requested the usual information, details of my vessel, the planets we had transited in the last six Earth months, bios for my crew, (just Skrog and myself), and our vaccination status for COVID 2090. He also asked for credit account verification for the fuel and supplies we would buy. I pressed my left palm, with its implanted chip, on my scanner and sent what he required.

I decided to express my thoughts: "Your docking rig looks a little old. Have you experienced any issues of late?"

"You'll be fine. Your ship isn't too big. You won't have an issue."

"You didn't answer my question. Any problems recently?"

It was obvious that he was about to lie, but he paused and must have realized I was going to demand the truth.

He looked away but said, "We had a pleasure craft from Earth a few weeks ago. They weren't very skilled and didn't make their coupling properly."

"And?"

He hesitated. "They crashed."

"Casualties?"

He hesitated again.

I repeated, "Casualties?"

"They all died."

I was becoming more worried. "Are you the senior docking agent?"

"No."

"Is that person available now?"

"Maybe."

"Hey, I don't want to be annoying, but I'm uncomfortable with this. If I can't have the senior docker work his tethering magic, I'm not docking."

He paused again and then said, "I'll see if he wants to take over. It's his break period and he hates having that interrupted."

"I'm hovering in position to berth, so make it quick."

Skrog wobbled back and forth, an expression I knew to be the equivalent of a human shaking his head.

It was clear that the planet's response would take a while, so I decided I had time to recheck the fuel levels of the ion thruster propellant. The nuclear pile would last forever, but the thrusters required an additive, and it was that that was low. If we chose not to land and refuel, could we make it to the next fuel depot, a space station in orbit on the other side of Mars?

The gauges showed a level of 3% and this told me that the answer was probably not.

I indicated the dials to Skrog and he again wobbled, "Like not, Cap."

My thoughts were interrupted by a call. A different, taller, bearded man appeared in the hologram.

"This is the Senior Docker. What do you want?"

"I'm a little concerned about your recent accident, and I wanted to have the best person assisting me with docking."

While waiting, I had consulted a system-wide directory. "Your name is Mup Plom isn't it?" He grunted and I lied. "I have heard such great things about your expertise, track record, and experience as a true professional in managing the docking maneuver." I crossed my fingers.

The man grunted again and I saw he was swaying a little, "I'm just back from my break. Do you really want me to do this?" It was obvious that he had been drinking.

I persisted. "Guess you observed the accident with the pleasure craft." I was starting to fear the worst.

"Sure did. They were idiots. They called me back from my break to guide them in. Just like you're doing now. And then they couldn't understand my simple instructions." He paused. "Serve them right."

I thought leaving M1 and proceeding to the next fuel station would be tight with just 3% capacity left, but…

"Operations Command, connect pods."

Canot40 is a fuel depot on a space station orbiting Mars and our propellant additive gauge registered just 1% when we arrived there. Phew.

The station was newer than M1 and in good repair. It had been established when it became clear that refueling in space was more efficient than on a planet's surface.

But it was still just a fueling point known system-wide as a "truck stop". Cargo haulage people, like me, lived day in and day out in the void of space and considered anything better than the cabin of a tractor.

Although it had been built at a considerable cost, it was still a refueling station and the facilities were basic. However, the food was superior and more varied than that available on my ship and the station had hotel accommodations and an environment that did not require us to wear pressure suits. A little time here would be a welcome change, so along with the many other visiting haulage drivers, I regarded the fuel stop as an oasis in the great void of space.

I parked the cargo pods on a mooring buoy and navigated my craft to the fueling point. Refueling was easy and safe and I congratulated myself on my decision to avoid using the M1 facility.

"Skrog, let's stay over for a few days. Have a drink or two."

"Sound good, Cap."

I drove my ship back to the buoy, attached it, and removed my pressure suit since I would not require it on the station. It felt good whenever I removed the tight, rubberized garb and replaced the overalls that I wore under it with a fresh pair. They were black and old but clean. Skrog wore similar overalls, but his were bright green, which matched his skin tone.

We took our shore boat to the landing area, which was named Dinghy Dock.

Although Canot40 had been constructed to accommodate the expected growth in space travel by the end of the century, only nine spacecraft were currently moored at the facility. The newscasts pointed this out, along with situations in other underutilized outposts in the System. Despite this, people back on Earth still marveled that humans had "conquered" the universe. The World Council subsidized the operating losses of stations like Canot40.

The hotel, and its in-house restaurant, had installed a technology described as full Earth-like gravity. It was not quite as strong as on our home planet but better than on my tractor, which used a first-generation version of artificial gravity. Both, however, were much more advanced than the weightlessness experienced in early space travel. People have asked me how it works and my reply is that I have yet to learn. But it does, and I was looking forward to experiencing Canot40's version during my stay.

The facility boasted spacious rooms and suites and a large bar and restaurant that served alcohol, designer drugs, and food.

After checking in at the front desk bot, my number two and I entered the establishment and requested seating from the reservation terminal. We each passed our left palm over the scanner, and it accepted our identification. Seconds later, the system welcomed us.

I walked, and he slid, to our table, directed by floor lights. A robot replaced Skrog's chair with a larger one that they kept for his species. A window/screen showed, in real-time, Mars and its moons reflected in sunlight.

"That was lucky, Skrog. In a few hours, we wouldn't have had that view and would need to wait three days before it came back."

"Or," I added, "We could have requested a playback."

Skrog emitted a stream of air bubbles from his mouth in a movement like a human laughing. I have always called this "bubbling".

"Let's get drink, Cap."

"Money-wise, things are a bit tight at present, Skrog. I won't receive the first payment on the Saturn run for another two months. We'll have to stay with Galactic." I mentioned the brand name of the whiskey that was most prevalent in space at the time, something distilled on Mars. It was not very good but by far the cheapest.

"Understood, Cap. You need payments on tractor loan."

"Right. And did you see the cost of refueling the propellant additive? Inflation seems to be everywhere, not just back on Earth."

I did not bother to look at the drink options but said, "Order Command." A blue light flashed on the console, and I continued. "Two Galactics."

"Welcome Hut Mur. I assume you want Galactic whiskey. Is that what you want?"

"Yes."

A robot delivered them three minutes later.

I threw down the first whiskey as did Skrog and I ordered another round while perusing the food menu.

The restaurant had implemented Earth time and styled itself as a Mid-Western establishment. It had artificial buffalo heads on the walls, saloon-like swinging doors to enter the bar area, and robo-waiters dressed in cowboy and cowgirl attire. It used American Central Time, so the lighting and clocks indicated late afternoon and the choices were for an early-bird dinner. We made our selections, and I added a bottle of synthetic red wine. The wine wasn't going to be great but better than what we had on our ship.

I have never been a "foodie" and to me, the artificial beef rib we ate, tasted just as good as the real thing on Earth.

Skrog was a foodie. "Rib shit taste, Cap."

The voice recorder system at the table spoke. "Expletive detected. Skrog is fined $100. Shall I include this in your bill or do you want to pay it from a separate account?"

I laughed. "Recorder Command. Add it to my bill."

"Thank you, Hut Mur."

Chapter Two

You are probably wondering how I came to own a space tractor and be operating four hundred and thirty-five million kilometers from Earth. So, let's go back a little.

I was born in 2061 in a time of peace, prosperity, and growth on Earth. It was a period of change as, following the War of 2047, the planet had shifted to a global model with centralized government, and all countries had disbanded their defense forces.

Paralleling this, successive versions of COVID had caused a rethink on social intercourse. The virus has mutated annually since 2020, and the population has become conditioned to live, work, and learn from their homes. As such, I was enrolled in the standard schooling approach, a home-based, personalized, system called TESVG.

TESVG has been operating for nearly forty years and it addresses Training (practical aspects of life, using a wrist computer, using a Uni-cooker food preparer, hailing a robo-taxi), Education (scholarly stuff like art and literature), and Social skills (how to find friends, how to eat politely and so on). The final VG in the title relates to matching the individual with a job for which he or she is best suited - the Vocational Guidance module.

The student version of the hardware comprises a three-screen system with a single holographic adjunct operated from the pupil's home. Secure access is controlled wirelessly through each student's implanted chip.

The pupil works with the system which identifies his or her capabilities and interests. Recognizing that people can use different methods to learn, the interchange is personalized as it adapts to each individual. All lessons and interchanges are conducted remotely although there are some sessions in which multiple pupils are brought together in a holograph to foster social intercourse. Once every week or two, a play date is arranged for face-to-face contact between groups of students.

After years of one-on-one interaction, the system, based on its assessment of the student, recommends what career he or she is best suited for. That triggers job placement, which is also handled by TESVG.

My parents set up my parameters requesting a female voice and always talked about "her". I abbreviated TESVG to TES and called her Tes.

As with everyone else, I started my schooling at age three and the system provided tuition over the years until it judged that I was ready for full-time work.

Really intelligent students continue the process into their thirties, but most "quite smart" kids, graduate in their early twenties. Some leave the program as early as age eighteen and are known, disparagingly, as CNARS (Certainly Not a Rocket Scientist). This term was common and harked back to a time at the start of the 21st Century when spacecraft were driven by rockets and the people who designed, built, and flew them were scientists. These were scientists and often held "doctorates", a designation bestowed by "universities", which were the higher education institutions of the era.

When I was seventeen, TESVG commented on my poor grades to date and suggested that I might "graduate" the following year - a CNARS. I was incensed since I had worked hard on my studies and had, for the most part, enjoyed learning new things. I spoke with my parents about this decision by the AI system, and my father supported the TESVG conclusion saying that the system's integrity and predictive logic had been proven to be accurate for four decades. My mother was blunter. "Well, Hut. You must know you're not a rocket scientist."

I felt crushed and sulked for a few days but, realizing that I had no other choice, I accepted my fate.

To complete my studies and earn my diploma, I needed to undertake one major research assignment and report on my findings. Tes told me she would work with me on the project, but I knew that the system's testing and assessment of my skills would be inherent in this.

I spoke to the system. "What will the research be about?"

She answered. "Delta23."

The next day, I rose early and sat in front of my computer.

"Good morning, Tes," I said.

She, wirelessly, accessed the implanted chip in my left palm and verified my identity. "Good morning, Hut."

The system then followed up with the usual small talk which was common before starting the day's lesson. Then, she introduced the project that I needed to complete.

"We'll start with the development and implementation of the World Power Grid (WPG)."

"Wait. You said the project was about Delta23, not the Grid. What is Delta23 anyway?"

"Hut, I am the teacher, and you are the student. I shall tell you how Delta23 fits into the story when I decide to."

"Shit!"

Tes immediately issued a rebuke, advising me that when I left schooling using an expletive carried a fine of one hundred World dollars or more.

She then continued with her lesson. "The idea for the WPG or Grid, was first developed in 2045. It was simple and compelling. A grid would be constructed linking electricity generation plants and consumers in all countries across the planet. It would use 100% renewable energy based on solar and wind. In the daytime, when the sun shone in Australia, solar collectors, and the grid's superconductive wiring, could immediately provide New Yorkers with power, in the middle of the night, to run their home conditioning systems."

The system paused momentarily, and I quickly said, "Go on, Tes." I like to take control whenever I can.

"In 2049, after the War, scientists developed superconducting cables that did not require excessive cooling and started the construction of the Grid in 2050. Countries that had the most sun or wind, saw they could become beneficiaries as suppliers. A small island in Polynesia installed a vast solar field and experienced exponential economic growth as did the windiest country on Earth, Antarctica. Cities like Manhattan bought the power but generated little of their own. Just as Worldnet allowed access to information from anywhere, the Grid provided electricity to everyone. Any questions, so far?"

I shrugged and Tes continued her lecturing.

"It was a huge undertaking, and it took fifteen years to install the high voltage undersea and in-ground cables linking supply and demand. New laws were enacted to allow corporations and countries to provide and use the service. The system was regulated by the World Electricity Council and energy consumption was made available inexpensively and with a minimal tax."

I was becoming bored with her monolog and asked, "When does Delta23 make an appearance, Tes?"

She ignored my query and continued. "Early in the project, there was a problem. If it was raining in Australia, or the wind did not blow in Antarctica, there might not be sufficient power generated in real-time for the evening requirements in New York or elsewhere." Tes posed a question. "So, Hut, how did the Grid solve this issue?"

I did not need to be a rocket scientist to answer. "Batteries," I replied.

"Energy storage systems." She corrected me, but I knew my reply was good enough to earn me some points.

She lectured me on how the batteries of 2050 used an antiquated technology and that a new solution was needed to support the Grid.

"How was that issue resolved, Hut?"

I was stumped, particularly since I was conducting this interaction with TESVG in 2078 and the Grid had been running for the past sixteen years. It started operations when I was one year old. How would I know when all this had happened so long ago?

My hesitation indicated that I did not have an answer, so Tes said, "Hut, Look up article reference ZDZ-148263"

I called to my wrist computer. "Wristcom On."

I spoke the article reference number, and my computer accessed the document and displayed it on one of the TESVG screens. It described a metal that became the heart of a new battery technology developed in 2055. The worldwide energy storage issue was solved. However, it still did not answer my question about how Delta23 fitted into the story.

2055? I thought back to what I had learned about that year.

It was seven years after the short, but devastating, World War 3, and Earth was still recovering. The War had come close to eliminating all of Earth's lifeforms and the shock of this reality prompted an awakening across the planet. Decisions on what was important, and what was not, were uppermost in people's minds. Previously, governments had been dysfunctional at the national and state levels, and these traits contributed to the conflict. Expanding from the moribund United Nations, a world government was established, and, while not perfect, it provided greater stability and was regarded, by most, as worth the gamble. One of its first steps was to compel countries to abandon their defense forces and armament programs.

I did not know, at the time, the role that aliens played in this transition.

The new world government recognized a need for optimistic ventures to improve the population's morale so it turned to major space projects to provide this. They made huge investments in nascent but advanced technologies and funded a few small colonies on Earth's moon, followed by bases on Mars and even on Jupiter's largest moon, Ganymede.

I returned my attention to the article and saw that, in 2050, mining companies started exploring the Asteroid Belt between Mars and Jupiter hoping to discover planetary bodies which were rich in metals and minerals. They gambled that these could be mined economically, and the ore shipped to Earth. The dream of an asteroid that was

100% pure gold was compelling. The World Council divided the Belt into quadrants labeled with names from the ancient Greek alphabet and added numbers to indicate specific asteroids. One key player, mentioned in the exploration, was a corporation called China Mining. Interesting.

I asked Tes, "Tell me more about China Mining."

TESVG released a sound like a mechanical chuckle. "It was a minor, mining company. Excuse the pun!"

I groaned. At times, the personalized nature of the system was infuriating.

"Continue, Tes."

"China Mining had been a force in Chinese metal extraction and refinement for years and, as space travel became viable, asked the World Court for access to metals and minerals on other planets, particularly Mars. The court denied this but as a consolation prize, gave the company rights to any ore found and exported to Earth from any planetary body in one, named, quadrant of the Asteroid Belt.

"Hey, Tes, I am becoming frustrated. You were telling me about battery technology. What's the Asteroid Belt to do with that."

"Patience, Hut. Keep reading a little more."

I did so and identified a section about a particular asteroid. Bingo!

Tes interrupted my research with a soft but excited voice. "Yes, Hut, one of the asteroids was called Delta23."

Tes returned to her normal lecturing tone.

"Delta23 is an unpopulated rock that is about one hundred kilometers across. China Mining discovered it in 2051 and discovered that it was primarily composed of an unknown metal on Earth. It seemed to have some unique characteristics and without much imagination, the commander of the mining exploration vessel and her chief scientist named it Delt, almost the same name as the asteroid. So much for scientific originality."

The system paused so I asked, "And?"

TESVG continued. "China Mining sent samples of the new metal to a dozen manufacturing companies, and most found that it served no purpose. One, however, Battery City Enterprises, located in what was then called Detroit, recognized its properties as a rare earth substitute, nearly perfect for a new battery technology it was developing."

I put Tes on pause and started some research of my own. Accessing ten or twelve press articles about the negotiations between China Mining and Battery City, I saw that both had played some sneaky tricks when negotiating the supply of the unique metal. Later, Battery City launched an acquisition bid for China Mining, resulting in the purchase of the company and its off-Earth assets for a fraction of what they would later be valued. The merged operation renamed itself World Energy Corporation.

I was starting to enjoy my project, so I continued to read about China Mining and its development activities on Delta23.

The company funded an operation on the asteroid to mine the ore and early studies indicated that it would be less expensive to refine the impurities from the raw material on the asteroid before shipping it to Earth. They built below-surface refineries to extract the pure Delt and the metal became the major component of the electrode in every future battery manufactured.

I liked researching on my own but after a few hours, I grew impatient and decided to have Tes do the heavy lifting.

"Tes, what happened after the mining and refining operations were completed?"

She let out an electronic gasp. She accessed my wrist computer, and I knew she was monitoring my research work. I was delighted since my independent studies should have gained me some credits towards graduation.

Tes showed her excitement. "When refined, the metal was smelted into ingots, stored, and subsequently shipped to Earth. A space tractor and its captain, visited Delta23, loaded ten cargo pods with the Delt, and in a single voyage, transported all that was required for the entire Grid network and, later, for all other Earth batteries - for vehicles, computers, communicators, everything."

I queried Tes. "What's a space tractor?"

TESVG gave me the sound I associated with an electronic shrug, implying that she believed everyone should know this. Nevertheless, she provided an answer. The hologram displayed a large robo-truck with a string of containers attached driving at speed along a North American highway. "On Earth, a lot of freight deliveries are still by road, and semi-trailers, also known as tractor trailers, are employed. The tractor provides the haulage power and the trailers carry the cargo. This has been the case for more than a century."

She paused to ensure I was still paying attention. "These days, the road tractor is self-driving, and it tows one or more trailers, filled with goods."

The image changed. "A space tractor is similar and hauls pods loaded with cargo from one part of the Solar System to another." The hologram showed a spaceship with a string of pods trailing behind it.

Tes continued. "Although flying a space tractor is mainly automated, the World Council demands that they have a human driver and co-driver on board."

I said to TESVG, "If the driver of this tractor shipped all the Delt to Earth, he must have made a fortune."

"No. Tractor drivers do not earn much. It's classified as a low-level job."

She directed me to more articles.

Having become the only supplier of Delt batteries, World Energy Corporation was authorized to build, and operate the World Power Grid. The company recruited the smartest scientists and became an elite organization and the largest company on Earth. By 2070, it provided electricity to nearly all of Earth's population.

One article caught my attention and I laughed.

In its haste to access the Delt, China Mining had mined and refined twice the amount required to manufacture all the batteries needed by Earth. Spending the time and effort to ship the excess metal from Delta23 to Earth, since it was not required, seemed pointless so the surplus supplies of the metal, in ingots, were left in piles on the asteroid.

I reported my findings to Tes, who commented, "You are doing well, Hut. But you have not asked me one particularly fundamental question."

"What?"

"I'll give you three minutes to work that out. Extra credits if you get it right."

I did not earn the additional credits.

"Alright, Hut, disappointing, but I'll tell you."

Tes simulated a sigh. "A most important aspect was how long the batteries would last. Batteries from previous technologies degraded across their life until, at a certain age, they had to be replaced."

I nodded my understanding, "I'll bet the Delt batteries had a short life."

"Wrong, Hut. No one knew how long they would last, but early testing indicated no degradation and World Energy released a forecast that they would be operational for one hundred years or more. The initial batch also included spares, providing sufficient capacity for no further manufacturing to be needed for at least eighty years. No new batteries have been built after the first batches. Those in place have operated flawlessly and have required no maintenance or repair. An outstanding success story."

"Tell me more about the way the battery technology was developed, Tes."

"Of course, Hut. This was a major job for a specialist team of scientists."

"How did the scientists go about their work?"

She told me more about the process, and I found the information fascinating.

I spent the next two weeks finalizing my research and, upon its completion, I constructed a holographic, video presentation summarizing the key aspects. I checked my work, smiled at how good I thought it was, and presented it to Tes to earn my graduation.

I waited to hear Tes's response which came faster than I had expected. How did she have the time to assess all the effort I had put in?

She appeared in the hologram, depicted as a mid-forties woman, wearing a cap and gown.

"Well done, Hut. You missed a few points, but you have captured the most important aspects of the Delta23 story. I hereby graduate you from TESVG and am awarding you a final score of a B minus."

My 3D printer started and created a certificate on thick parchment with an embossed ribbon and language indicating my graduation at age eighteen. Although not stated on the certificate, I was well aware that this designated me a CNARS.

I had hoped for a B or, perhaps even a B+ but a least I had graduated.

"So, Hut, has the Delta23 story given you any ideas for your future career?"

I was excited. "Absolutely. I love it and I know now what I want to do."

"Ok, what do you want to become?"

"A scientist."

"A scientist, Hut?"

"Yes, Tes, a scientist."

The system paused. "I have another idea, Hut. Why not be a space tractor driver?"

Tes offered me a discounted, post-graduate course on space flight, tractor architecture, and space navigation. When I completed these, she arranged an apprenticeship on a space tractor for four years, and at the end of this time, I was promoted to captain. I worked for a freight forwarding company for another two years until, at age twenty-five, I took out a loan, purchased a secondhand tractor, and started my own business transporting cargo.

It was a lonely life, with months between seeing other humans face-to-face. However, the holo-call system allowed me to keep in touch with my few friends back on Earth and, overall, I loved the work. But I was about to encounter people and events that would lead me on an adventure and answer the question I posed in my book's Prologue -where would I end up?

Chapter Three

Skrog and I finished our meal on Canot40 and were drinking another round of whiskies when he started to bubble. I looked at him and noticed his middle eyes looking beyond me, further into the restaurant. "You missing something, Cap."

I looked around the room which was about a quarter occupied and saw her. She was sitting alone at a table at the rear and wore a single-piece designer suit in silver that clung tightly to her body. Her hair was cut short and was colored a light red, a fashionable color in 2091. She sat erect and seemed to exude intelligence. She was tall, with a trim figure and an angular face. Perhaps it was the effect of the Galactics, but she appeared a little blurred. She was beautiful.

I guessed that she was about my age—30 years. She was nursing a frosted blue drink as she perused the food menu.

Skrog bubbled another laugh. "Took you long, see her, Cap."

"What do you mean?"

"She in nine minutes ago. You not notice. For nine minutes. She pretty by Earth standards. Yes?"

"Damn it Skrog. If I had six eyes with each pair focused on a different range, I would have seen her immediately."

He bubbled. "She alone. What is girl without mate doing at truck stop? She not a tractor driver."

I laughed. "Not dressed like that she's not." By then, I had drunk several Galactics and felt I was the master of the universe. "I'm going to say hi." Rising, I nearly stumbled, but regained my steadiness and walked to the girl's table.

"Hello, sweet thing. I'm Hut. Hut Mur."

She looked up and I noticed, for the first time, that she had amazing blue eyes. She wore white lipstick and a matching color on her fingernails. Perhaps it was the change of environment or maybe even the whiskeys, but as I took in the red of her hair, the blue in her eyes, and her white nails and lipstick, I thought of the old American flag. I smiled, but it came out as a snigger.

The blue eyes looked me full in the face. "So, Hut, what do you want?"

A thought flashed through my inebriated brain. I knew exactly what I wanted. But instead of telling her, I was smart and fed her a line. "I saw you sitting here alone and wondered if you needed company."

She sighed and returned her attention to the menu.

I was standing next to her table and realized I was becoming unsteady. It must have been the artificial gravity.

"Mind if I sit, sweet thing?"

"I don't want you to sit. I want you to leave. Do I have to call security?" Her finger hovered over a key on the menu system that would summon a robot.

"I'm sorry. I am. I'm so sorry. So sorry."

"Then go away and let me give you a suggestion. Don't call a woman "sweet thing" or any other derogatory term."

Swaying a little, I knew I needed to leave her, but was unsure if I could make it back to my table.

I turned and nearly ran into Skrog. He had joined us and now addressed the woman.

"Hello. My name is Skrog. Apologize captain here. I take him away from you."

"Thanks, Skrog. At least there's one gentleman in this hellhole."

He guided me back to our table and as we sat down, I said to him, "What does derogatory mean?"

He bubbled. "English not my language, Cap. How would Skrog know?"

My wrist computer held the answer: "Wristcom on." It flashed blue, indicating it was listening. "Tell me what derogatory means."

The system spoke quietly. "a term expressing disrespect."

I gazed up at a six-meter wall screen showing the void of space with an array of stars and then turned to the menu system. "Order Command. Another Galactic."

At 6:30 A.M. the artificial sunlight "streamed in" through my hotel room's window/screen and I groaned. Galactics always affect me, and I vaguely remember drinking five in the restaurant and perhaps one of two more after Skrog carried me to my room at the station. Based on his size and mass, he had been given a special suite, larger than most, that was reserved for people of his species.

I spoke into the intercom. "Connect Skrog."

"Morning, Cap."

"I feel terrible. Must be something I ate last night. I'll see you in the restaurant in half an hour."

I showered, shaved, put on the overalls I had worn the previous day, and met Skrog for breakfast. Looking around, I noticed the girl sitting, still alone, at another table. She now wore a light green tunic over a darker green body suit.

"I'm going to apologize," I told him.

He bubbled. "Her name is Flama. Flama Omm."

I wondered how he knew this as I rose and started walking towards her. Suddenly, I felt unwell and had to change course and rush to the bathroom. As you know, rushing with limited gravity is not very attractive. I bounced across the floor, narrowly missing a seasoned trucker with transparent patches in his overalls, revealing the tattoos on his skin below.

I decided to give up on Flama Omm and returned to my table. I said to Skrog, "What do you think? Shall we skip the next day or so here and get back into space?"

"Good by me, Cap."

I accessed our bill and passed my left palm over the scanner. The system read my implanted chip.

As I paid, I focused on the total bill and remembered something I had learned in Social Studies History from Tes. They had some crazy things going on back in the early part of the century. The world, led by what was then called the United States of America, embraced a rampant tipping mentality. It reached an expectation level that even robots expected a gratuity of 40% or more. Weird.

Then a court case ruled that tipping was the equivalent of bribery and bribery was illegal. Several people who left tips were indicted. People accepting tips were separately found guilty of taking bribes - corruption. In landmark cases, several were convicted and sentenced to large fines. All the vendors, who had supported the idea that their employees should be paid directly by their customers, changed their processes overnight and tipping became defunct, just another silly idea from fifty years ago.

As I was rising to return to my tractor, I looked up and saw Flama approaching. What does she want?

She stopped and smiled—a lovely smile displaying a full set of sparkling white veneers—expensive veneers. Her body suit and tunic were slim-fitting, showing off her figure, which was worth showing off.

"It's Hut, isn't it?"

"Er, yes. That's right."

"I wonder if you can help me." She gave me another big smile.

Flama's story sounded unlikely, and I didn't know whether I should believe her or not.

She told me she was a biologist traveling on a TESVG grant to study several herbs that grew, without water, in the hydrogen-rich atmosphere of Jupiter. Following the research, she would write a lesson module on her findings. She had arranged passage on a space tractor, like mine, for the trip from Earth but while in transit, the tractor captain received an urgent cargo request which meant he needed to return to his base in New Beijing. He dumped his passenger on Canot40.

I motioned her to take a seat. She continued, "I understand that you are leaving for Saturn and will be passing Jupiter. Any chance of taking a passenger and dropping her off at Jupiter Station?"

"Passenger? You?" I asked.

She was smiling again but her expression seemed to say, "Yes, me. Who, the hell, else, moron?"

Instead, she said, "Yes. Me."

I looked at her. "It's somewhat out of my way…"

She hid what was a clear sign of annoyance that I was not eager to welcome her on board but continued, "TESVG has provided a substantial level of expenses for the trip, so I can pay you well."

I thought about it. I had a loan payment due in a few weeks and would be pressed to cover it. The deposit for the Saturn ice contract would not be available by then, but Flama Omm could solve my short-term problem. As I named a price, Skrog looked at me and blinked all six eyes, implying that he knew it was much higher than usual.

Flama looked at me with those beautiful blue eyes and said quietly, "The fare seems excessive, but I have little choice. When can we leave?" Then, she reached out and touched my arm. I felt a pleasant electric tingle run through my body, and I pulled away from her. From the look on her face, she might have experienced the same tingle, but I was probably projecting.

My reaction, to her request for passage to Jupiter, should have been more positive, but something in the back of my head told me that this trip would not be straightforward. Perhaps I had just been in space alone and away from humans for too long. Maybe I saw how attractive this woman was and worried about how I would handle her proximity for a week or two. The electric tingle had been wild!

I made up my mind. "Okay. We'll stay the night here on Canot40. Leave first thing tomorrow morning."

<hr />

After dinner, that night I sat with Skrog in the bar and watched a newscast from Earth on one of the restaurant's huge screens.

As usual, there was a group of commentators railing against the World Council's ban on the personal ownership of firearms. This had been led by Americans and going on for decades. It was accompanied by an argument to swing away from globalization to more local government administration. After the War, the consolidation of governments globally resulted in most legislation being determined by global bodies rather than by individual countries or regions and some people did not like this. Before, many decisions were made at the country or even at the state level. Some even more locally. Counties? Townships? Crazy stuff!

It is hard to imagine that the States of North America comprised three separate countries which was the case until 2049. Yes, Mexico, the United States of America, and Canada had different constitutions, different laws, different currencies, and even different languages. The United States encompassed fifty states, each of which had significant autonomy and, often, enacted conflicting legislation. At least when the three countries merged, the World Council recognized that the term "United States of America" was a misnomer since the states were far from united. They omitted the word "United" when the North American block was established and named.

Newscasts mostly stayed the same, day-to-day, but one small article caught my attention. The newscaster spoke in his usual animated fashion. "Germany, a little over a week ago, experienced a power outage that lasted nearly an hour. When we asked for comments from World Energy Corporation, which manages the World Power Grid, they shrugged off the failure." He continued, "The fifty-minute outage is the first since the Grid started operations twenty-four years ago. A spokesman told us that a team of scientists was investigating and that no other services were affected. The impact was local to a small region west of Frankfurt, Germany."

He sat at his desk with four so-called experts beamed in from various parts of the globe. "Let's find out the reactions of our experts." The screen split to reveal the faces of his panel members and he asked them., "What's your take on this? Is this something we should be concerned about?"

The first, a well-known fashion influencer from Paris, jumped in. "This is just a little blip. We'll have all forgotten it by tomorrow. Unlike the new, in color – light green…" My mind remembered the tunic Flama had been wearing.

Another, a political commentator based in Lima, Peru, introduced a more alarming interpretation. "I have no proof yet, but my sources tell me that this is the first in a larger plot by the terrorist state of Arabia."

An older woman from Athens, whose credentials included writing a multitude of papers on the politics of the ancient world, interrupted him. "That's stupid. My people tell me that it was a disgruntled employee who sabotaged a battery array. Probably one of the arrays at the Grid's headquarters in Greenland."

Another, who had been a resident panelist for over a decade and specialized in healthcare suggested, "Perhaps, COVID 2090 has infected the Grid in some way." He added a sound bite, "Bugs in the Grid", hoping that would be picked up by the other networks.

I changed feeds and put the news out of my mind.

Though I can reliably, tell you about all the events when I was present, others happening on Earth, or elsewhere in space, impacted the story. As I was writing my narrative, I needed a way of capturing these and feeding them into my manuscript.

I turned to my old tutor, Tes, and used my wrist computer to connect with her site.

"Hi, Tes."

"Hello, Hut. It's been a while."

"Yes."

"Have you been well? How is the job working out?"

"I'm fine but I need your help."

"Let me check your records." A few milliseconds later, she continued, "Got it. You have a paid-up alumnae status, so fire away. What can I do for you?"

"I'm preparing a book about my adventure in 2091. Many things were happening at the time, but I wasn't present for a lot of them. Is there any way I can research that?"

Tes gave me her electronic chuckle. "A book? Writing was not something you were very good at." She paused for effect before continuing, "But, this is exciting Hut, and I have your answer. The World Freedom of Information Act."

"What's that, Tes?"

She shifted to her lecturing mode, which had previously annoyed me. However, I had matured, and I listened intensely.

"In 2080, the World Supreme Court completed an extensive study investigating nearly a million law cases as part of replacing human lawyers with AI bots. It found that most outcomes, in both criminal and civil suits, were based on the recollection of conversations between people, and many of these were shown to be erroneous, misinterpreted, or overt lies."

Her monolog seemed to need to be more relevant. Tes, please focus on what I need."

She ignored my request, as she did during my earlier schooling, and continued. "The Court concluded that an accurate reporting of the dialog between humans would have allowed a better course for justice in over seventy

45

percent of cases. The justices mandated that all future discussions, worldwide, be automatically recorded."

I interrupted her. "I know all that. I put up with it every day. Particularly if I drop a swear word."

Tes said, "Correct. One of the justices introduced that idea since if they were recording all conversations anyway, they could check for swearing and issue fines accordingly. A great gesture to the conservatives and a significant money maker."

She poured out a deluge of facts about the voice recorder system. "The shift to universal recording provided a huge revenue stream for a corporation in Argentina that developed the technology, provided the recording equipment, and hosted the information storage. The Chief Justice of the World Court, coincidently, was Argentinian."

"Tes, please get to the point."

She gave me her electronic shrug. "Participants were allowed to categorize their dialog as personal and when they did so, the information was held securely and only the participants had access to the recordings."

"So?"

"The World Freedom of Information Act made transcripts of conversations, which related to business or government, available to the public. There are some exceptions for security issues, but transcripts of most discussions can be accessed."

Now her monolog started to make sense. I smiled. "I can see where you are going with this. I'll be able to access the relevant conversations when I wasn't present."

Tes's hologram chuckled. "In 2087, a follow-up study revealed a significant number of conversations that were business/government had been deliberately miscategorized as personal to avoid access by the public. The Argentinian voice recording company was directed to add analysis modules to their system that would review the content and alter the classification if necessary. After that, a trove of information became available for any individual who had the interest and skills to locate pertinent transcripts."

"How do I access the transcripts, Tes?"

"You're in luck, Hut. I have a special course on that very subject. And I can offer you a discounted price…"

I decided to access the transcripts and then provide my readers with summaries of the most relevant ones. As I started writing my manuscript, I changed my mind and decided to include the transcripts themselves. More authentic!

The first is a meeting held at the World Power Grid headquarters a week after the German power outage. The participants were a Grid executive and a Grid scientist. The recording/transcription system is imperfect; sometimes, it replaces individuals' names with generic titles or redacts them altogether.

TRANSCRIPT - WPG-10147-38297
World Power Grid (WPG) Headquarters
Nuuk, Greenland
January 20, 2091/1:12 P.M.
Classification: Originally marked Personal - recoded Business

Grid Executive: From your report, I see that we now have nineteen failures across the Grid.

Scientist: That's right, sir but apart from the first one in Germany, we've managed to keep them secret.

Grid Executive: So, NAME REDACTED, what have you found?

Scientist: We don't have conclusive proof yet.

Grid Executive: Understood. But what did you find? What's causing the problem?

Scientist: It's the batteries.

Grid Executive: The batteries?

Scientist: Yes. They appear to be failing.

Grid Executive: Failing? How are they failing?

Scientist: They have stopped retaining charge.

Grid Executive: Then fix them. Aren't they being maintained?

Scientist: They have never required maintenance.

Grid Executive: Get someone to fix them.

Scientist: No one knows how to do that. All the batteries needed for the Grid were manufactured twenty-four years ago and have been operating flawlessly all that time. No maintenance was needed. No failures."

Grid Executive: Explain.

Scientist: In 2056, World Energy Corporation manufactured all the batteries they thought they needed for the Grid. In the next few years, the technology was adopted for all other batteries - land vehicles, airplanes, boats, computers, and communicators. When a device needs to be replaced, the old battery is transferred to the replacement. Our scientists expected them to be serviceable for at least one hundred years, and there was no need to manufacture additional units. No one alive today worked on the design or the manufacturing process.

Grid Executive: There must be documentation. Videos? Holos?

Scientist: Most of the documentation is on incompatible media. Systems that stored data back then used hardware devices that have been superseded. I have people working on converting the information to current technology.

Grid Executive: Get it fixed, NAME REDACTED. So far, our system capacity has allowed us to operate smoothly, but if these batteries keep failing, we'll have a catastrophe on our hands.

Chapter Four

On Canot40, Skrog and I enjoyed our last evening meal on the station and after a few more Galactics, I decided to turn in for the night. The next morning, we had an early start and my thoughts returned to the passenger we would have with us on our flight to Jupiter. She was attractive and seemed easy to get on with in our meeting a day earlier. But I had a nagging suspicion that the trip might not be plain sailing.

My experience with women was limited, and spending twenty-four hours a day on what would be a ten-to-twelve-day journey with one would be something new.

Hey, what was I thinking? She was just a fee-paying passenger. She could have been seventy years old. But Flama Omm was not seventy years of age.

As I mentioned, my tractor has three cabins, one specially equipped for Skrog, one for me, and a spare, so accommodation for a single passenger would be fine. She had conducted her research on our flight plan, and with the orbits well aligned, it would be an easy diversion to land her on the small Jupiter station.

I settled our bill at the hotel by passing my left palm over the scanner in my room, but something was unsettling about the mysterious woman, so I called Skrog.

"I'm not sure about Ms. Omm. Verify what she told us."

"Understand, Cap."

Ten minutes later, he called and told me what he had found. "Not much online, Cap. Graduated recently, age 31. Smart. Very smart."

I started pacing about my room. "I've not had a lot of experience with women, Skrog." Well, there was the sex worker on Saturn6 and a couple of brief liaisons when on vacation on Earth. I continued, "Women are just so different to guys. What's your take on her? Do you trust her?"

"My experience Earth women less than yours. She strong. Intelligent. But honest? Not know." He added, "Expensive clothes and wrist computer is top-of-line. I checked credit. Odd. She has a Platinum chip implant but scores just average. Most credit balances high but fine for fee agreed. Solves your loan payment problem."

As Skrog, Flama Omm, and I were preparing to shuttle out to my tractor, another meeting was taking place on Earth.

TRANSCRIPT - WEQ-10294-2017
World Power Grid (WPG) Headquarters
Nuuk, Greenland
January 30, 2091/9:11 A.M.
Classification: Originally marked Personal - recoded Business

Grid Executive: We've dealt with over one hundred failures so far, and the Grid is still holding. The public is still only aware of that first outage, and our PR people handled that well.

Scientist: True but this is not a temporary issue. As more batteries fail, we'll move closer and closer to, perhaps, the greatest disaster the world has ever faced.

Grid Executive: You're the scientist. What's the answer?

Scientist: My team and I found what we believe to be the problem.

Grid Executive: Then spit it out.

Scientist: It's in the batteries. The Delt metal, which is the heart of the electrode, has become depleted.

Grid Executive: Nonsense. Delt batteries were thoroughly tested back in 2056 and certified to have a life of over one hundred years. All the press releases and WSEC filings were clear that the Delt would not need a replacement for at least a century—perhaps never.

Scientist: The scientists in 2056 got it wrong. Think about it, sir. How could they know how long they would last? It was new technology and a new metal. They were guessing. Or they wanted to satisfy the government watchdog agency. Or drive up Energy's stock price.

Grid Executive: How can you fix the problem?

Scientist: If we had fresh Delt, we could swap out that module, which should give us another 24 or so years. We would have time to develop a newer technology. Hell, sir, I am 70 years old, and you are older. I'm up to retire in five years. We'll both be dead by the time the next management team faces the issue.

Grid Executive: I understand. But it's not just the Grid. Delt is the heart of every battery on Earth. World

Uber will come to a grinding halt. My wrist computer will stop working.

Scientist: Not yet. The Grid batteries were all manufactured and installed first. That was a few years before the technology was implemented in other battery applications - vehicles, computers, boats. We can expect all those batteries to last another two or three years. In the meantime, if we can acquire new Delt we can swap out the Grid batteries and roll out the others as an "upgrade". No one will know the difference.

Grid Executive: How do we get more Delt?

Scientist: According to the notes, it is just waiting for us on the asteroid Delta23.

"Welcome on board, Flama Omm," I said enthusiastically as our shore boat docked at my tractor. She had already put on her pressure suit, which was designer-grade and well-fitting. Normally, pressure suits resemble the wet suits used over the past century and are rarely flattering. Her suit appeared to be brand new, and although it was not designed to accentuate her curves, it did so, nevertheless.

We passed through the airlock, and as Skrog unloaded her baggage, I noticed that our new passenger had traveled with significant luggage. Skrog proceeded to secure the shore boat for the trip to Jupiter, and I showed Flama around my ship.

I was not expecting to have a visitor, so I had not cleaned up the living space, as I probably should have, but I am a tidy man, and Skrog is quite fastidious. The areas were clean and litter-free.

My craft, however, was not a pleasure vessel and, tractors are tractors.

Flama had told us that she had traveled on one previously, so I did not expect her to be surprised by the utilitarian accommodation that she found.

She looked around and pouted. "This ship is really old. Is it first generation?"

I had been happy to take her on board, but I was already questioning my decision. "It's third-gen. Well, second-gen, but with enhancements."

"It's so worn."

"It's only twenty years old. It's a tractor, not a pleasure craft. Everything works, it has some special features and I've enhanced a lot of the technology."

We were standing in the lounge at the time and looking around, she shook her head. "Is this the only lounge area?"

All I could say was, "Yes."

"It's so small. And there'll be three of us." I could see she was also thinking of Skrog's size.

"Flama, you've traveled by tractor before. Or that's what you told us. These vessels are all quite basic."

She looked up at me. "True but the other one was a fifth-generation vessel and equipped for up to six passengers plus the crew. In addition to the two pilots, it had two stewards. Human not robots."

"We don't have a steward. Robot or human."

She had carried a small bag with her and her main luggage was still in the hanger. She ran a finger over the top of a cabinet. Checking for dust? She shook her head. "I'm not sure this will do. Let me see my stateroom."

I laughed at her use of the term "stateroom."

"Your cabin is over here." I took her to one of the several doors leading from the lounge area which had the number three in raised letters at eye level.

"Does it have a bathroom en suite?"

"Of course."

We entered the room where she would sleep, and her beautiful blue eyes surveyed the space. She frowned. "Small, isn't it?"

"The bed is King large, and you have a hanging area in lockers around the room. The windows/screens are all along the outside wall and you can program them to give images the equivalent of a normal window or you can use them as monitors for your wrist computer or other communications. You can watch videos in your cabin or the lounge."

"Holo-calls?"

"Yes. We have personal holo-call capability in every room on the ship. Except for the bathrooms, of course. The commercial-grade system is in the Control Center."

"Exercise and workout?"

"Of course. It's the standard. Built into the bed. You lie down, issue a voice command and the system attaches your arms and legs, stretches you, and works all your muscle groups. It also provides cardio."

"I know how they work, thank you."

She took a few steps to a door leading to her bathroom, opened it, and looked inside. "Miniscule, isn't it?" Before I had a chance to answer her, she asked, "It uses water? An old-fashioned shower? Not an AirClean?"

I answered, "Yes, it uses water. But I do have the AirDry system."

In the past half hour, I had been wondering whether taking Flama Omm to Jupiter was a good idea. She was showing a bitchy mood which could make the trip unbearable. My mind now changed. I no longer wondered whether it was a good idea, but now concluded that it was certainly not a good idea.

"Listen, Ms. Omm. The facilities on my ship don't seem to match what you need, so let's not pursue this further. I'll drop you back on Canot40 and you can find a more suitable form of transport. Perhaps a private Speeder."

I realized as I was saying this that I had an imminent loan payment due, but I was sure that the passage to Jupiter would be hell if she remained on board.

"Are you kicking me out, Hut?"

I shrugged. "Yep. I guess I am. I'll have Skrog reload your bags and we'll ferry you across to the station."

She walked to the shower and said, "Shower Command." A blue light flashed, and she continued, "Turn on water. Full pressure."

A torrent of water poured out of the shower head and she said, "Shower Command. Off." She looked at me. "Good water pressure." Placing her carry bag on the bedside shelf, she bounced on the bed. Looking around, she put her head to one side and seemed to make up her mind. Ignoring my earlier statement, she said, "I think this will be just fine. Thanks, Hut."

I was about to shout at her when the thought of the pending loan payment flooded my brain. Anyway, what could go wrong? I was captain of the ship and I was in charge.

I sighed. "Okay, let's check you in. I need to verify your identification, medical, and the rest. Your chip is in your left palm, I assume."

"That's right"

I shook my head. "And we need to set you up on the voice recording system."

Her eyes were magical, and I could not help but look at this attractive woman. We would share a small spacecraft for many days, and I wondered, again, if I had made a mistake in agreeing to ferry her to Jupiter.

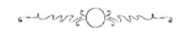

Skrog brought her main luggage up to the cabin and I left for the Control Center.

I spoke. "Operations Command." A blue light flashed. "Attach cargo pods to our ship and disconnect them from the mooring buoy."

I watched the screen as we prepared to cast off.

When the pods were in place, I issued my next order. "Navigation command."

Nothing happened.

I shouted at the system, "Navigation Command," and the blue light flashed. "Set course for Jupiter Station. Most direct route."

Navigation replied in her French accent. "Bonjour, Hut. What safety level?"

I paused. "Safety level eight."

Skrog's two outer eyes swiveled to look at me. "Not safety level ten, Cap?"

"Eight is fine. We'll get a notification if there's an issue."

"Path takes through Asteroid Belt. Could be problem."

"I don't want this trip to be any longer than it must be. I want that woman off my ship. We took a risk bypassing M1 and flying on to Canot40 and I'm happy to take another risk now."

"Understood, Cap."

The voice of Navigation Command interrupted. "Course calculated, set and Operations Command notified."

"Estimated duration?"

"Eleven days, four hours and twenty-three minutes."

Skrog motioned towards the lounge where Flama was making herself at home. "You not like her, do you?'

"No. I don't think I do."

We engaged the engines and set off. After my initial skirmishes with Flama, I decided it would be best to lay out some ground rules.

We met in the lounge and I did not waste any words. "Skrog and I will operate as previously. We each work twelve-hour shifts, and one of us is always awake and able to make quick decisions if they're required." The ship's AI systems made most of these assessments automatically and our role was largely superfluous. "Ms. Omm, you have unlimited use of the lounge and your cabin, but you need my permission to enter the Control Center." The look from Skrog showed me he could not understand why I was restricting Flama in this way. I told him later that I wanted to ensure that he and I had some space away from her if we needed it. I added to Flama, "You will not, at any time, enter the engineering or thruster areas."

Flama gave me a sickly smile. "I am a paying passenger, and the ticket price was exorbitant. I shall keep to my stateroom most of the time, but you will serve me my meals, and clean my room to a schedule that we'll agree. And if either of you makes a pass at me, I'll have you charged. You'll spend the rest of your miserable life in a penal colony. I'm told the one on Saturn is the worst in the solar system."

I tried to think of a smart reply but could not think of one, so I gave a huff and returned to the Control Center.

Modern tractors are generally well-equipped and built to include the comforts that a small crew wants for long, boring flights with little human contact. We had an extensive collection of video equipment in most rooms, with communication channels to allow personal holographic connections with people on Earth or wherever.

Those on board can use the same social media systems that currently occupy humans for about 70% of their waking hours. The sales pitch from the tractor salesperson who sold me the craft was that, since most people spend less than 10% of their time in face-to-face contact with others, being alone in space, millions of miles from home, is similar.

Let me tell you. It is not. You cannot go for a walk outside, visit a restaurant, or play a sport. But the pay is quite good, and the bragging rights are huge. "Hey babe, I'm a spaceship captain."

You get used to the solitude and adapt to the life of a recluse. One negative side effect is that after about a year in space, most crews feel uncomfortable among people in even lightly crowded environments. Most people who fly on a spaceship even for a short trip, a week or two, easily accept the change. I quickly discovered that Flama was different from these.

The first day passed uneventfully. Flama kept to her cabin, joining Skrog and me for meals. We ate simply at lunch. Skrog and I each had a sandwich while she opted for a salad. Our first dinner was one of my favorites - grilled chicken.

I placed the prepared dishes on the table and smiled at her.

"This, Ms. Omm, is one of the best meals available on tractors."

She glared at me. "I'll be the judge of that, Hut." Having said this, she seemed to relax a little. "And you may call me Flama."

She was obviously hungry and tackled the meal aggressively.

"Hmm. Not bad."

I smiled. Perhaps, she would be an okay passenger after all.

Skrog had laid the table in the dining area and we sat there when we ate. Flama looked about and appeared to find the venue surprising.

She angled her head towards us and asked, "Do you always have meals at the table? I thought you would have it on your laps on the couch and watch newscasts or sports videos."

I tried to decide if, in Flama's view, she found this positive or not. I answered her question truthfully. "Yes. We have all three daily meals sitting here at the table. It was something that I was taught as a boy, and I've carried the tradition with me into space."

Skrog added, "Food eating social. Hut and I discuss events and ideas."

I turned the question back on Flama. "So did you and your parents eat at a table?"

She looked away and quietly said, "Yes." Then she returned to eating and sipping a glass of wine, that I had poured for her.

The second day, Flama came into the lounge wearing another outfit, skintight leggings with a skirt in matching gold. To me, it was a little formal for our basic tractor, but I refrained from commenting. Perhaps, she was going to parade different clothes every day just to push me for a comment that she could shoot down.

That evening, as we were having dinner, more grilled chicken, I mentioned. "Skrog and I are going to be busy tomorrow. We'll be transiting the Asteroid Belt in the afternoon, so you'll have to get your own breakfast."

"I'll manage. Oh, and I like the chicken, but two days in a row?"

I sensed that she was unhappy with the environment, and perhaps Skrog and me. Then she shook her head, rose, and erupted. "This ship is the smallest in the Solar System. There are no people to talk to. No one to do my hair, my nails."

I narrowly avoided rolling my eyes.

She glared at me "Don't look at me like that."

I was taken aback. "I wasn't."

She continued. "We both know that salons on Earth are all robot staffed and the robots are the ones who provide the services. But there are always other human customers to talk to."

I answered her. "You have us. Skrog and me."

"Nothing personal but you, Hut, are so obviously a CNARS. Skrog is smarter but still. And you're both males. I want to talk with other girls."

"You can do that on BodyTime. Use the system in the privacy of your cabin. Call your friends and have holo-calls with them."

Flama looked away. "It's too late now. I'll try them tomorrow."

Surprised, I asked, "Where do they live? It's only 8 p.m. America Eastern Time. Or even earlier on Western Time. Or are they in some other country?"

She paused. Her hesitation lasted longer than it needed to and I realized that she regretted starting this conversation. Then it hit me. I said, "You can't answer because you don't have any friends, do you?"

She snarled at me but did not reply. Without another word, she turned, walked quietly to her cabin, and closed the door behind her. I heard the magnetic lock being applied.

I helped Skrog clear the table and put the plates and flatware into the Uni-cleaner. He activated the appliance and, pouring myself a Galactic, I settled down to watch a video. A few minutes later, Flama emerged from her cabin and answered the question I had posed earlier. "No. I don't have many friends."

I couldn't help asking, "Not many or not any?"

She snapped. "God, I could hate you."

"God" is not legally regarded as an expletive, so the voice recorder did not issue a fine.

I softened my tone. "Listen, Flama. It's not a problem. I don't have any friends either."

She let out a snarl. "That is understandable."

We both lapsed into silence, and I wondered where the conversation would go if it even started again. Skrog rose and headed toward the Control Center.

Flama said quietly, "When I was growing up, I spent all my time on TESVG and graduated at the top grade level. But I flunked out on the social modules. My theory tests scored great, but I failed the practical ones, like Friends 101, and so on." She grimaced. "I'm sorry. This is not the real me. Guess I'm just tired."

I asked her, "Want a drink? I have whiskey or gin."

She looked strangely at me and noticed, for the first time, the Galactic I was holding. "I thought you weren't supposed to have hard liquor on spacecraft."

"Well, Flama, on this spacecraft, we do. Gin? Or wine?"

"Gin."

I poured a Galactic Gin for her.

"I don't drink much."

"Now may be the time to start. Tonic?"

She shook her head, took the glass without requesting a mixer, and gulped the drink down. Her blue eyes widened, and she let out a shriek as the raw spirit burned her throat. "God, that's awful."

"Galactic is not a premium brand."

She looked at the empty glass in front of her. "It certainly isn't."

I asked "Refill?" She nodded and I poured another drink for her.

As I did so, I could not help but notice how well her custom pressure suit clung to her body over the latest designer clothes that she wore. She was an attractive woman and those eyes…

She interrupted my thoughts. "What do you call your ship, Hut?"

"What do you mean?"

"When you talk about it, what do you call it?"

Where's this going?

"I call it 'ship'. Or 'tractor' or 'spacecraft'. What else would I call it?"

"That's not what I mean. People always name their vessels. Before robo-taxis, when people had their own land vehicles, they gave them names. Lady Bug. Big Blue. This is a spaceship so you might call it Celestial One or Advantage 37. Something personal. Or after a partner - The Lady Penelope."

I had never thought about it. "I guess people might have some personal relationship with their ships, but I don't feel that. It's a tractor. It gets me and my cargo from coordinate A to coordinate B. I call it 'ship.'"

"That's appalling." She drained her glass emitting another small gasp at the taste.

I looked at her. "Why?"
She muttered, "Soulless." and held out her glass again

Chapter Five

Early the following day, Flama emerged from her cabin, and it was clear she was suffering from a monstrous hangover. She wore her clothes from the previous day, no pressure suit and her hair was disheveled.

"God. I feel awful." She looked about the lounge area and I could see a thought formulating. Then, a cloud drifted over her face.

She turned to me and pointed an accusing finger. "Did we?"

I answered nonchalantly. "Did we what?"

"You know what."

"No. I really don't know what."

Actually, I did know what.

"Did we have sex?"

I was about to respond, but my inner childishness took over. I decided to show her who was in control of my ship. So, I paused and looked thoughtfully at her, rolling my eyes, until she grabbed me by my pressure suit collar.

"Answer me, you asshole. Did we have sex?"

The voice recorder interrupted. "Expletive detected. Flama Omm is fined $100."

I smiled at her. "No. We didn't. I don't have sex with women who have passed out."

She searched my face deciding if I was telling the truth and made up her mind.

"Okay." As an afterthought, she added, "Thanks, Hut." She moved to return to her cabin and spoke in a cracked voice. "I don't feel well. I'm going back to lie down."

I scowled. "You need to put on your pressure suit."

"Why?"

"You know why."

She looked down at what she was wearing. "Why aren't I wearing it from last night? Who, the fuck, removed it?"

"Flama Omm is fined $100."

"I was worried that you might throw up if you kept it on, so I asked Skrog to remove it. We were going to wake you after it had been off for five hours. That's the protocol."

She grunted and entered her cabin closing the door behind her.

A half-hour later, she emerged wearing her pressure suit, though I could tell that she hated it. Under it, she wore a light blue bodysuit.

She looked at me. "You got me drunk, last night."

"No. I didn't get you drunk. You got yourself drunk."

She relapsed into silence, accessed her wrist computer, and threw the image of a newscast up to one of the wall screens. She adjusted her earpiece to the program and gazed at the screen trying to show interest in it but I could tell she just wanted to avoid looking in my direction.

I needed to join Skrog in the Control Center but paused and asked her, "Don't forget. You need to get your own breakfast today, Flama."

"You must be joking. The mere thought of food makes me nauseous."

I walked to the kitchen area woke up the Uni-medic and said, "Hangover relief for Ms. Omm."

"Coming right up, Captain."

The system checked Flama's medical records, which it had uploaded from her implanted chip when she came on board. It then churned for a few seconds before delivering a small dose of pink liquid into a glass.

I offered it to Flama. "Drink this."

She gave me her withering look, that I had now seen often, but took the glass and swilled it back. "Yuck."

I took the empty glass from her. "We'll be entering the Asteroid Belt in about two hours, so I'm going through to the Control Center. If you change your mind about breakfast, help yourself."

Skrog and I normally spent little time in the Control Center other than for official holo-calls. Generally, we sat in the lounge, and if the system needed us, a speaker would alert us and request that we go to Control. This was our typical mode of operation, but I noticed that since Flama had come on board, Skrog had spent more time in the Center than ever before.

I left Flama and joined him in Control.

"When do we reach the Belt?"

He turned and said, "One hour, Cap."

"I notice you're spending more and more time here, not in the lounge. Why is that?"

"Well, Cap, you and Flama always arguing. Bad. Skrog not happy."

"Gosh, old buddy, I can't help it. She drives me mad with her whining the whole time."

The woman was exasperating. And I still didn't know much about her. Her past was a mystery but why would I care about her earlier life? Her money was good and we only had another eight days before we arrived on Jupiter. I groaned. Eight days. Eight 24-hour days!

A reminder from the navigation system bleeped and I checked the screens and the automatic pilot. Everything seemed in order.

"Navigation Command," I said, and once again, it did not flash. There was no response.

I spoke louder and more clearly.

"Navigation Command." Navigation woke up, flashing her blue light.

I shook my head. "Anything I need to be aware of?"

The French voice answered, "No, Hut. This is information only. A small asteroid swarm will pass within four thousand kilometers but have no impact on our flight course."

Although I knew the answer, I asked, "Navigation Command. When will we reach Jupiter station?"

"Eight days, six hours, and forty-seven minutes to docking."

I glanced at the controls, and everything seemed in order.

I turned back to my number two. "Skrog, have you noticed? Every time I ask Flama about herself, she finds a way to deflect the question. She doesn't seem to want to tell us anything about her earlier life."

"Agree, Cap. She hiding something."

A mechanical voice punctuated the quiet. "Random drug and alcohol test, Hut Mur and Skrog hold sensors." I looked at my wrist computer and noted the time: 9:06 A.M. It was still morning, thank goodness.

We each shrugged and took a sensor from a shelf. We waited a few seconds while the system analyzed our state of sobriety. "Drug level zero. Alcohol level zero. Both Hut Mur and Skrog pass. Thank you." I laughed. If it had been 9:06 in the evening the result would have been different.

Our passage from Mars to Jupiter through the Asteroid Belt presented the greatest threat of danger in our journey. Outside the Belt, there are a few meteors and space debris that need to be avoided, but the Belt comprises many more hazards. Skrog and I always stayed alert, taking turns in the Control Center during our transit.

The ship's autonomic systems were designed to handle the situation, projecting asteroid paths, sensing possible danger, and avoiding it. The computers worked flawlessly, and no effort was required from us, but I have always been a cautious man, and getting just one thing wrong would result in a collision and certain death.

For security purposes, there is a lockable door between the Control Center and the lounge and although we had not locked it, the door was closed. In the early afternoon, there was a knock and, since both Skrog and I were in the Center at the time, it was, obviously, Flama.

I glanced at Skrog and four of his eyes looked away.

I grunted. "Come on in, Flama."

The door opened, and she entered, looking around. She seemed to have recovered from her hangover and had changed into pink, loose trousers with a blouse in a darker shade of the same color. I noticed she was not wearing her pressure suit.

"Good afternoon, Skrog. Afternoon Hut."

She had not been in the Control Center before and took in the technology that was installed. "It's quite old tech, isn't it?"

I already regretted allowing her in. "It serves the purpose."

She kept talking, reaching toward one of the screens, and I stopped her. "Don't touch. And you should wear your pressure suit."

She withdrew her hand. "You don't have any outside windows, do you?"

"No. Why would I want that? I have a hundred cameras so I can see out without having the risk of a window malfunctioning and leaking. The images are clearer, and I can magnify them and view different angles."

She pouted. "It's not the same though."

I shrugged. She was starting to annoy me again and could probably read the irritation on my face. Perhaps she was trying to goad me.

She gazed at the display console and uttered what sounded to me like a snort. "Space travel is so boring with just the blackness of space and rarely even seeing one planetary body. Going through the Asteroid Belt, as we are now, should be much more fun but just watching these screens isn't particularly interesting."

I decided to humor her. "I do have a full 360x360 degree hologram."

"You do?"

"That's what I just said." I already regretted telling her about the system.

The previous owner of my spacecraft had installed it just before selling me the ship. He made a point of mentioning it as a feature. I saw no real value in it and had never used it in my five years of owning the tractor.

She looked at me with those blue eyes. "Hut, can we run it?"

I looked over at Skrog who blinked all his eyes, indicating he could set up the system easily.

"Okay, Flama. Skrog will pipe it through to the lounge."

I rose, escorted her there, and indicated the two armchairs that would be optimal for the experience. We each took one and settled back waiting for Skrog to activate the system.

Flama showed her signature impatience. "When will it start? Or is it broken?"

Suddenly, the walls and furniture faded away, replaced by a hologram with us in the center. The hologram spread around us, above and below. It displayed the scene outside the tractor as if we were sitting in space. Even the armchairs that we sat in seemed to disappear.

Flama gasped and let out a cry.

The first time you see this type of hologram, it takes your breath away, and initially, you fear that you will fall or drift off into the void. A minute or two later, most people think the wonder of the sights all around them is mind-blowing.

"Oh my God. It's beautiful." She was over her initial fright.

Thousands of asteroids flew past us as my tractor negotiated the swarms of them. The majority were only a meter or two across, but their physical composition reflected light sending a rainbow of colors that sparkled and changed continually.

Flama was absorbed and marveled at the views of the myriads of rocks flashing by as we passed them. Now and then, a larger planetoid came into view and although I enjoyed the show, I could have been more impressed. It confirmed my assessment that this was a useless feature for a space tractor.

I identified some of the named, planetary bodies.

Then, my final TESVG project about one of these rocks, Delta23, returned to my mind. I consulted a chart app on my wrist computer, which indicated that the mysterious asteroid was on the far side of the belt at the time and would not come into view. I did not know, at the time, that I would soon be venturing onto that lump of a planetoid.

After about twenty minutes, Flama appeared mesmerized by the show, but I got bored. We were gazing out at the splendor when Skrog's voice broke through from a speaker.

"Big problem. Control Center now, Cap."

Flama showed her surprise. "What's happening?"

I spat out the words to her. "I'm going to find out."

She stamped her foot. "I'm coming with you."

"No, you're not."

"Yes, I am."

I let out a sigh of exasperation and said sharply, "Alright, but I'm in charge of this ship and I don't want any suggestions on how to do my job. If you come, you stay silent. Alright?"

"Okay."

"Skrog, kill the hologram."

I moved quickly to the Control Center and took my place in the forward seat. Flama sat behind me and I imagined her eyes darting over the display screens.

Skrog did not wait for me to ask him. "Navigation detect five meteorites heading intersect our path."

"Big ones?"

"Two meters each and very fast. Puncture hull if hit."

"Avoidance plan?"

"Many asteroids all around us. Limits what we can do."

"Risk level?"

"Navigation says threat level nine."

As I had expected, Flama could not keep quiet. "What are you going to do? If one hits us, we'll all die."

"Shut up. I'm thinking."

She opened her mouth to speak again but this time Skrog said. "Flama. Shut mouth."

She did so.

I spoke. "Navigation Command." Thankfully the blue light flashed. "Show projections of paths of all asteroids and meteors related to possible collision." As I said the word "collision" Flama let out a wail.

The system responded. "On screen, Hut." Navigation presented a picture of every rock around us, projecting its future path.

"Navigation Command. Plot path for us to avoid strike."

The French voice answered calmly. "None available, Hut."

"What do you mean? None available?"

"My analysis shows that there is no path you can take to avoid a collision."

"Not acceptable. Find one."

"As I said, Hut, avoidance is not possible. There is no path available. My calculations are valid." Her calmness was starting to grate on me.

I looked at the screen and took in what the system had just told me. It looked grim but I had been a tractor captain for over ten years and had learned that sometimes the artificial intelligence Navigation system did not consider variables outside its comfort zone.

Leaning forward in my driver's seat, I replayed the projected movements and then replayed them again. The system was correct in its analysis. We were in imminent danger. But an idea struck me.

"Navigation Command. Load these coordinates and flight plan."

"I already have a flight plan, Hut."

"Don't argue. Delete your plan and accept this."

I rattled off a string of maneuvers for the ship and instructed Navigation to update her projections. A second or two later, the display changed, and the maps showed the revisions and their impact.

Skrog was watching closely and bubbled. "That work good, Cap."

"Navigation Command. Link to Operations Command and Implement."

"Implementing, Hut."

The tractor executed a sharp turn to the right and flew to a position one hundred kilometers shielded by a medium-sized asteroid. Our cargo pods straightened into a line behind us as we came to a complete stop. An asteroid was between us and the meteorites.

"Hut. What are you doing?" Flama's query incensed me.

Skog said sternly, "Flama. Shut mouth."

The screens reflected the maneuver and we waited to see if my solution would work.

Flama was about to speak again when Skrog turned to her and focused all six of his eyes on the woman. It was threatening, and she closed her open mouth.

A few minutes passed and then our screens showed the meteorite swarms passing by. Three others struck the asteroid we were hiding behind but not us. There are no sounds from collisions in space, so we watched, in silence, as the asteroid was devastated by the impact of the meteorites and several dozen pieces of it exploded around us.

I gasped. "If you're religious, Flama, it would be a good time for a prayer that one of those fragments doesn't strike us."

I looked over and it was clear she was not religious. She sat there silent with a shocked expression on her face.

Nothing happened immediately so I ran a new simulation and it projected that we would not be hit. The pieces from the fractured asteroid spun past us as I had hoped.

"Navigation Command. Are we clear?"

"Yes. The path is now clear, Hut."

Flama was motionless, staring at the screens. Perhaps this was one of the few times I ever saw her speechless.

I exhaled and then Navigation spoke. "Hut, why did you not accept my analysis? Your override avoided the issue. My calculations were valid but did not solve the problem. You did not use my intelligence for your solution. I do not understand."

"Sometimes, Navigation, it comes down to a human's gut feeling and going for a simple approach rather than a complex one. Hide behind something bigger. Being a CNARS can be a positive."

Flama gave me a stony look that I couldn't read. Was she upset that we had come close to death or thankful for my resourcefulness in saving us?

Chapter Six

Skrog and I spent the morning of the fourth day in the Control Center but returned to the lounge for lunch. Flama was sitting in the armchair she had claimed on the first day of our journey. She wore yet another outfit, this one with purple highlights. She turned to face me, and I braced myself for an expected string of complaints or sarcastic comments. Instead, she appeared to have calmed somewhat and requested something I had not anticipated.

"Hut, tell me about your family."

I considered her request and concluded that telling her about my upbringing might ease the tension. If I told her about myself, she would feel obliged to tell Skrog and me more about her own life. Despite my negative feelings towards the woman, I was interested in her background, as was Skrog.

I settled back in an armchair and started my story. "My birth was normal. My mom and dad completed the child-bearing exam, passed, and applied for a license. It was granted so they contributed their seeds, and these were introduced into a standard artificial womb. They watched me grow and after nine months, on schedule, they were both present when I was born. Or this is what they told me. I was, of course, already fully immunized, checked for telltale signs of potential deceases later in life, and so on."

"Chip?"

"Implanted in my left palm," I remembered that Flama had a platinum chip, whereas mine was stainless steel.

I thought about the old-fashioned pregnancy process and shook my head. "It's amazing, isn't it, Flama? For millennia, and even into the first half of the current century, women had to carry a child inside their bodies, feeling it grow for three-quarters of a year, and then endure the pain of giving birth."

She swept a hand through her hair. "You know that a significant number of mothers in some class D countries, still do it the old way. Very inconvenient, very painful, and it has inherent health risks for mother and child." She looked away. "What's appalling is that even in class A countries, for nearly twenty years, women, and some men, were against the use of the technology saying that it broke a bond in families. Women thrived on the closeness and even the discomfort of carrying a child. Religious leaders also fought it thinking it was against God's will."

Skrog wobbled. "So primitive. My people switch external wombs centuries ago."

I directed a question to Flama. "I assume you had a similar birthing. Right?"

She ignored my question and nailed me with another query. "Are your parents still alive? What jobs did they have?"

I felt compelled to answer the woman. Perhaps it was all those years in school with Tes. Growing up, I had been taught to reply to questions. So, I replied to her: "Both are still alive and working. Dad is in climate insurance, and Mom is a zone manager for Amazon."

I found Flama's inquisitive tone annoying but adopted a tactic I had used with Tes. If I kept talking, she would not have a chance to interrupt and I would take control of the exchange. "Along with most of the population, my parents worked from our home as I was growing up. Each had a small separate office room as was demanded by their employers, and each traveled a few days a month to a meeting center where managers and colleagues bonded and did face-to-face socializing. And of course, daily, they used the normal remote video conferencing or holographic systems."

She interrupted my flow. "Where did you live?"

It was clear that my tactics would not be successful, so I gave in. "We had a home in suburban Albany, New York. My parents and brother still rent there."

"Tell me about your brother."

"He's five years younger than me and an AI programmer. Still lives at home."

"Transportation?"

Although increasingly frustrated by the interrogation, I could not think of a way to avoid answering her questions. "Same as most others. We used World Uber. We didn't have a personal vehicle if that's what you're asking. We just used robo-taxi services. Our house was new, so we didn't have the type of garage that they still have in homes built before mid-century."

I tried to redirect the conversation to her. "So Flama, where did you grow up?"

She looked at the watch area on her wrist computer. "Gosh, it's late. I have a call with a work colleague scheduled shortly. I'll skip lunch, and let's pick it up later."

I did not believe her.

Flama returned to the lounge at the time we usually had dinner. She had changed and wore a turquoise bodysuit under her pressure suit.

She looked around and made a show of choosing a path to avoid one of the armchairs, indicating that she, still, regarded the area as being small.

I was wearing my pressure suit over my normal overalls, and she picked up on this.

"Is your only outfit a pair of overalls?"

I grimaced. *What now?* "Yes. Why?"

"I've only seen you in that same pair."

"I have three pairs. All like one another and all the same color. Deciding what to wear each day is easy."

"Three pairs the same?"

"Yes. I wear a fresh one every day and I clean two at a time every second day."

"Men!" She shook her head and scowled at me. "What's for dinner tonight? It had better not be grilled chicken, again."

I sighed. "No. We are having grilled fish."

"What type of fish?"

"I have no idea." I picked up a package from the food locker and read the label. "It says 'Wahoo'. It's an Earth fish."

"I know that. There are no fish in space."

"Skrog. What do you think? Wahoo tonight?"

"Yes, Cap. Add herb. Preserved lemon. Ginger. Delicious."

I unwrapped the three frozen, single-serve packs and placed them in the Uni-cooker while Skrog searched for the herbs, lemon packs, and ginger root.

I spoke to the appliance. "Cooker Command. Defrost fish." The blue light flashed, and the appliance hummed for a few seconds.

"Done, Hut."

Skrog slid forward and taking the fillets from the machine, coated them with a mix of vacuumed thyme and basil, ginger, which he ground using an electric grater, and the preserved lemon. He then looked through our food locker and removed some green beans and potato sticks for the sides.

"I cook, Cap?" he asked.

"Sure."

He bubbled. "I do manual."

Skrog loved cooking the old-fashioned way, and I have to confess that his approach always made the food taste better than the "fully automatic" function of the Uni-cooker.

He spoke. "Cooker Command. Preheat grill."

"Done."

He placed the food onto separate areas in the spacious appliance and said, "Cook."

The Uni-cooker detected the various foods and grilled the Wahoo while steaming the green beans. It also air-fried the potato sticks. Within five minutes, each was cooked to perfection—well, I would call it perfection. Skrog, the foodie, was always critical.

Flama sat at the table and attacked her meal. "Not bad. Better than the chicken. But Skrog prepared this meal, so I can understand why it would be better."

Skrog bubbled. I hissed at her.

The next morning, day five of our journey, Flama came into the lounge area and was clearly in yet another bad mood.

"I am getting claustrophobic. Is there anywhere else I can go to walk around a bit? This is a big ship. There must be somewhere."

Skrog offered a possibility. "Look at engines?"

I was about to veto this suggestion when Flama replied, "That sounds like it might work."

She turned to me. "Surely you can't have an objection to that."

I sighed and nodded my acceptance of the excursion. "If we do this, I want to clarify one thing. The engine room is a dangerous place. We'll take you there, but you must obey all instructions from either Skrog or me. Is that clear?"

"Yes, sir, Captain!" Her sarcasm did not make me feel any happier about our little side trip.

Gesturing towards the Control Center, I said, "Skrog, take the lead."

When we had entered the Center, Skrog issued a command. "Elevator Command. Open."

A section of the floor slid aside, and a structure rose into the space. It revealed a single-person open elevator.

Skrog pointed to the platform. "Flama. Do what Skrog does."

He slid onto the platform and used additional voice commands to take the elevator down before returning the empty structure to Control. The convenience was designed to cope with someone of Skrog's size and weight, so when it returned it would have been possible for Flama and me to squeeze in together. But I smiled at her and said, "You're next."

She entered, spoke the same commands she had heard Skrog using, and descended.

I waited, wondering if she would decide not to send the elevator back for me, but it arrived, and shortly afterward, I joined the pair of them fifty meters below in a small room with several doors opening to various elements of the engineering facility.

Skrog opened a door marked "Engine" and we slipped through it to a grated, steel catwalk that extended over one hundred meters between the two ion thrusters. "This is what powers us," I explained to Flama, although I'm sure she had already deduced this.

Skrog bubbled and pointed to a large adjacent area with a transparent tank filled with an orange liquid. "Propellent based on Martian technology. Passed to Earth in 2049. Basis for how to explore space."

I confirmed what Skrog had told her, but she gave me a withering stare that implied she believed him more than she believed anything I might tell her.

She started forward along the walkway and I called to her. "Be careful. The artificial gravity doesn't work as well here, and the catwalk can be slippery. If you fall, you'll drop several hundred meters and die."

Her reaction did not surprise me. "Ha."

Skrog interjected. "Flama listen. Hut words good."

She turned and walked quickly away from us without holding the rail.

I called to her. "Hold the rail."

"I have excellent balance."

The tractor's ion thrusters operate consistently but, now and then, the navigation system initiates a course correction, and the engines either slow down or speed up. The thrusters mimic the change and vibrate a little when this occurs. The artificial gravity system cuts out for a second or two. Not a big deal, but…

The thrusters accelerated, and the engine room shuddered a little because of the vibration.

Flama Omm, standing on the side of the catwalk, experienced an instant without gravity. She let out a cry and pitched forward, falling. She landed on the structure out of reach of the handrail and found herself lying only centimeters from the edge. Full gravity returned.

She uttered a shriek and tried to scramble further onto the catwalk but, in doing so, slid backward towards the abyss. Skrog started to move to her as we both saw Flama's predicament. His movements based on sliding his twenty or so toes on each foot, were slower than was needed to save her so I shouted to him. "Skrog. Get out of the way."

He realized that he was standing in my path and, coming to a halt, initiated a movement I had not seen before. He rolled to his side and allowed me to crawl over him to get to Flama.

From her prone position, she had been unable to find anything to hold onto, and her efforts to move toward the center of the walkway had the opposite effect. She was starting to slide over the edge.

She let out another scream but as she did so, I reached her, grabbing her arm as the lower part of her body slid into space. She screamed again. I held her but knew that as she struggled, it was likely that she would pull me over as well.

For a moment, the thought that, maybe, I should just let her go, ran through my head. It would certainly make the trip a lot more enjoyable, but the paperwork would be enormous. As well, she still owed me the second half of her fare and her implanted chip would automatically cease to operate if she died.

Skrog had righted himself and slid over to us. He extended his left arm and grasped Flama by the collar of her pressure suit, easily lifting her back to the gallery and me along with her.

He wobbled. "Okay?"

I nodded, and Flama just sat there staring into the void, marveling that she was still alive.

I gave her a severe look. "Party time is over. Back to the lounge."

When we were passing through the Control Center, she looked at both of us and in a quiet voice said, "Thanks. Thanks for saving my life." She added, "Thanks for putting up with me." Then, she vomited, narrowly missing the main console.

<hr />

Flama retired early that night, and the next morning, day six, she appeared in another outfit, a pair of half-length trousers and a skintight blouse. The trousers were a dark red and the top a lighter shade of the same. She was not wearing her pressure suit.

Skrog greeted her. "Good morning, Flama. What you want breakfast?" She smiled at him.

She did have a beautiful smile. But she had never smiled at me. Well, maybe she had once or twice back on Canot40 when she wanted me to agree to take her to Jupiter.

Skrog continued, "You normally fruit and cereal. If prefer, I make bacon and scrambled eggs."

"Just cereal, please. No fruit today."

He slid over to the food locker, selected a mix of fourteen-grain dried pellets, and withdrew some milk from the preservation unit.

She ignored me as he set down her breakfast and addressed him. "I've never met a Martian before. It must be a challenge working with humans." She gave me her withering look. "Particularly, some of them."

I had hoped that the adventure in the thruster area might have mellowed Flama. I did not doubt that she regarded Skrog as the one who had saved her and not me.

Skrog bubbled. "I not Martian. Earthlings call us Martians but we not Martian."

I was sure that Flama knew this but she waited for him to continue.

"Mars is where we live now. Lived there last two centuries. Original planet was…" He then spoke the name of his home world, including a harmonic screech and a bass guttural grunt. It is unpronounceable for human speakers and impossible to write. Flama started to form the word with her mouth.

I sighed. "Don't even try to say it. I've tried for years, and it's just not possible for Earthlings."

She gave me a look that said, If you were not a CNARS, you might have had better luck.

She turned back to my short, round, green shipmate. "Skrog, say it again."

He did so.

She attempted to emulate it but was unable to do so.

He spoke the name again and she tried again.

After multiple attempts, Skrog bubbled. "No human can say."

"Can you Anglicize it?"

"Planet name is holy to my people. We not translate to other languages."

"Oh. I'm sorry."

Skrog had been sitting on the couch but now, rose to stand looking slightly down on Flama and me. "Scout ship from my planet located Earth long time ago. Original home world devastated by meteor swarms. Needed new home for race and tried many planets. Your world was best fit. We found Earth."

Flama leaned towards him "That was back in the twentieth century. 1914, wasn't it?"

He bubbled at her interest. "Yes. Earth year 1914."

Her eyes opened wide. "Nearly 200 years ago?"

"Correct."

She continued. "But no one on Earth knew about your people for one hundred and fifty years after that."

"True. Except later. Our scout ships were observed. Earthlings called them UFOs."

"Why did it take so long for humans to find out about your presence?"

"We kept secret."

"Why did you do that?"

"Gravity of your planet and level of oxygen in atmosphere not perfect for us so we needed evolve our bodies to cope. We use biotechnologies, but it still took one hundred years for evolution to occur."

Skrog sat again and added. "Also, we saw Earth at war within itself. Big war happening. We are peaceful species. Hope that after, your world settle into peace."

I decided to join the conversation. "That was called World War 1. It ended in 1918."

Skrog wobbled. "Correct. But we see that another war likely. We establish base on Earth's moon and observe. Clear to us that if we discovered, warring countries would regard us as threat and force us to fight them."

Flama frowned. "But if they attacked you, could you have defeated them?"

Skrog bubbled briefly. "Our technology makes easy for us to win, but waging war is against our culture."

"What happened next?"

"World War 2 and nuclear weapons. Then Earth start space flights. Earth could discover us. Home planet nearing its end, so we moved large population – one hundred thousand – to new base in hidden underground cities on Mars."

Flama asked another question. "What about your home world?"

Skog wobbled violently, underlining how hurtful the memory was. "Destroyed. No longer option return there. We only people left and either stay on Mars or move to Earth. He continued, "Then World War 3."

Flama shook her head. "That only lasted for six months."

Skrog countered, "Yes but it nearly result destruction of human race."

"It was fairly local. Between India and China."

While I had not enjoyed many of my studies with Tes, warfare had been an area that fascinated me. I said, "It started that way but even that was significant since these two Asian nations comprised 40% of the world population. Four billion people. Then more countries became involved. North Korea launched an attack on Hawaii, which was then part of the United States. Half the inhabitants there were killed."

I knew that Flama was aware of the history but decided to spell it out to show her that I was not as stupid as she seemed to think. "The United States retaliated against North Korea with a directed missile strike, and the other countries recognized the overall threat level of a nuclear war. India reverted to a land-based assault using conventional methods and within six months, had won a huge tract of China but with significant losses. After a series of negotiated cease-fire agreements, the War terminated. The Indian Supreme Commander, at the time, commented, 'We gave the lives of over one million of our troops and conquered territory that we had already destroyed. We also lost nearly one million civilians. The battles gained us a thousand square kilometers of rubble and cost us two million citizens.'"

Skrog wobbled. "Clear to us, another accidental war likely destroy Earth, and no chance we have new home. In 2050, our High President arrange secret meetings with Earth leaders and make ultimatum. Abolish war. Centralize power globally. Solve disputes through government or judiciary. High President issued threat if not accept."

Flama leaned forward. "I didn't know that. Was it accepted?"

"Yes. Your planet feared us. We make small demonstrations of our aggression weaponry. Scared them shitless."

"Expletive detected. Skrog fined $100."

"We offered trade to allow us move to Earth. World leaders agree and we provide technologies including better ion thruster engines and additives for space travel but Earth never gave us land promised.

"You are saying that the shift to a World Government and elimination of country defense forces was driven by the…What do you call yourselves?"

"Call ourselves Martians now. Mars our only home so far. Yes. We drive these things."

I picked up the dialog. "After our world returned to peace, and accepted Martian demands to halt future military actions, the governments purged their generals and demanded a war-free environment across the planet. The United States created trade zones with Mexico and Canada and a few years later, these became one region, the States of North America."

I looked at Flama and saw she was surprised by my detailed knowledge. I continued. "All countries disbanded their armed forces over the next five years, and the World Guard was established to police illegal activities by terrorist and breakaway groups. The Guard answered to the newly formed World Council."

I rose and started to pace, but nearly fell over Flama's extended legs. I had never thought of our lounge as being small but perhaps she was right in her observation. "English, since it was the most common business language known to the world's population, was adopted as the official language of Earth. The World Court was also implemented, replacing the highest courts in each country. Shortly afterward, the jury system which had been in place for centuries was replaced by artificial intelligence-based bots that accepted all the evidence and issued a judgment as well as the sentence, if the defendant was found guilty."

As I said this, I noticed that Flama's face had hardened. "Verdicts could be appealed once with a more extensive AI system and finally, in some cases, the Supreme Court would hear a case. This court took evidence and arguments from the bots but comprised a panel of fifteen humans. Members of this judiciary were elected only by their peers who were other judges, avoiding any political affiliations."

I was on a roll so I added, "The World Court decided that each human was to have a chip implanted which would allow personal identification, online voting, replace licenses, access credit sources, make payments, and store health information. This was resisted by many fearing lost privacy, but the alternatives became more and more cumbersome, and, within ten years, most humans embraced the chip. Every newborn has one implanted at birth. The different currencies in countries were replaced by the World Dollar and became wholly electronic. Transactions using cash disappeared."

Skrog stood, walked over to the kitchen area, and requested chilled water from the Uni-cooker. "You see, Flama. Martians had big role in change on Earth."

I paused and sipped from my coffee. I had prepared it earlier, but now it was cold. I drank it anyway.

Skrog saw my empty cup and called the Uni-cooker to prepare another for me.

Chapter Seven

Flama settled back in her armchair as she seemed to digest what Skrog and I had told her. Then, she returned to her questioning. "How old are you, Skrog?"

"I am 120 years. My race lives normal 200 Earth years."

"You were alive when the War was in progress, then."

"Yes. Young adult and interesting time for a Martian."

I could tell that Flama was itching to ask her next question. And I guessed what it would be.

She leaned forward towards Skrog. "Have you encountered racial prejudice from the humans?" I was right.

It was an issue that I had asked him before and he had always given me a politically correct answer. However, from the way he reacted to Flama asking him, I detected that he might now be more forthcoming.

He bubbled and addressed her. "There always prejudice against beings different than you. You are woman and view men differently. Some humans have black skins, some brown, some white. Some rich, some poor. Some short and some tall." He burped. "This year, 2091, Earth has come long way valuing people what they are, what they do, and how likable. First Earthlings regarded my people as freaks. These mainly uneducated. Feared jobs. Position in society. TESVG not perfect but most humans now educated as best they absorb it…" I squirmed, "…and more tolerant. Odd. My people now less tolerant. Regard Earthlings inferior. I am very happy Skrog on this ship with you rather than in Mars colony."

Flama could just say, "Wow."

I interjected. "And what about you, Flama? What's your story?"

She brushed me off again. "I need some time to think about what Skrog just said. I'm going to lie down."

Each day that passed, I saw Flama in an array of different clothes. Sometimes, she wore a short tunic over trousers, sometimes a long flowing gown. They were all different colors and expensive. I wondered if she had eleven sets or more, one for each day.

However, one thing was constant. She continued to find fault with the ship and with me.

The evenings were the worst and followed a similar pattern.

I would ask, "Drink, Flama?"

"No."

"Water?"

"Yes. But it always tastes sour. Don't you have any fresh?"

"The water tastes that way because it is recycled and filtered. It is the purest water that you will ever drink."

"It tastes sour."

I continued to regret having agreed to her passage.

The next transcript sets out a meeting that occurred at the research department of the World Power Grid, six days into my flight to Jupiter with Flama and Skrog.

TRANSCRIPT - WPG-10320-41019
World Power Grid (WPG) Research Department
Nuuk, Greenland
February 6, 2091/1:12 P.M.
Classification: Originally marked Personal - recoded Business

Scientist 1: So far, the Grid is holding. But only just holding. Batteries are still failing but our capacity is such that we can cover it across the Grid with no service disruptions and none of our customers know that we have an issue. The other good news is that our tests indicate that introducing new Delt to the existing batteries solves the problem. If we can access a large enough quantity of Delt, we can swap out the electrode modules on all the batteries worldwide and everything will be back to normal.

Scientist 2: We can't afford any mistakes this time. How did you test your work?

Scientist 1: We found a small supply of the metal that was left over when the batteries were manufactured twenty-four years ago and, fortunately, it had yet to be used or discarded. It was in a museum in Old Beijing. The bottom line is that when we took one of the dead batteries and replaced the electrode component with one using the unused Delt, the battery returned to power and operated at 100% level. We used all the Delt we had and were able to reactivate thirty-seven batteries. They all worked.

Scientist 2: Do we know if the batteries will last?

Scientist 1: The test set showed no signs of depletion. The original batteries lasted 24 years so there is no reason to believe the replenished ones won't last for another 24 years. Replacing the spent Delt is the answer.

Scientist 2: And, if the stories are true, there's a huge supply of the metal on Delta23 and we need to get it to Earth?

Scientist 1: That's right, sir. Here are holo-pictures from 2057 showing the mountains of Delt ingots which were made at the time and not needed. We're sure, they're still there.

Scientist 2: Since China Mining quarried the ore and then refined it, and we acquired China Mining, the ingots are our property. Right?

Scientist 1: Well actually that is not necessarily the case.

We were four days out from Jupiter, and Flama had settled into a quieter mood. She was still critical of most things about me and my ship but was always pleasant when conversing with Skrog. I had decided to ignore her presence as much as possible, although since we all spent most of our time in the lounge, which was not that large, she and I continued to bicker.

It was 5:00 PM on the evening of Day 7, and she appeared from her cabin wearing yet another outfit—no pressure suit. She gave me a quizzical look.

I grunted at her. "Yes? What do you want?"

"Can you pour me a gin, Hut?"

I snarled. "I'm the captain of this craft, not a bartender."

She stiffened but did not reply.

I motioned to the shelf, "The gin is over there. Help yourself."

She did so and added a splash of basil tonic water concentrate and a lime cube. She placed her glass in the Ice Device, which chilled the mixture for her.

"Why do you hate me, Hut?"

"I don't hate you," I lied.

"Is it because you think I'm smarter than you?"

"Could be. You keep telling me you are."

"That's unfair."

"Not really."

She swirled the drink and took a sip. Her face revealed a grimace, and I knew she had poured too much gin into her glass. She added more tonic. Then, she looked at me and said quietly. "Do you want to have sex with me?"

I was sipping my whiskey as she asked this and choked.

She continued. "You've been giving me a look for the whole voyage and after that first night when I was drunk, I'm sure you've regretted that we didn't do it then."

I wiped the spilled whiskey from the top of my pressure suit and shook my head. "You just said that you think I hate you. If that's true, why would I want to have sex with you?" As I said this, I realized the weakness in my argument.

"Anyway, Captain Hut Mur, your luck is out. I'm not sleeping with you."

"I haven't even asked."

She swilled her gin down and poured herself another. I looked around for Skrog for support and remembered that he had descended to the main engine array to check some readings that the Autotester had reported.

I noticed that Flama had added very little tonic this time and wondered if she was hell-bent on getting drunk again. What is her game?

"What's for dinner, Hut? I'm paying you a lot for this flight. Well, TESVG is paying you a lot, but I am your only passenger and should be treated with respect. She is getting bombed!

I pretended to consult a menu screen. "Tonight, dinner comprises fourteen courses including many Earth specialties - shaved white truffles, fresh oysters, lobster thermidor, charcoal grilled steak, and several off-Earth delicacies - marinated Mars quadrapus, sautéed black tomatoes from Moon colony. These will be paired with some excellent wines from Europe France as well as other countries in the World Wine Collective. The vintage French champagne is unfortunately not available."

"Ha, ha." Her harsh response punctuated her reaction to my sarcasm.

I followed up. "It's grilled chicken."

"Not again."

"Grilled chicken is great. I love it."

"But for four meals in the last six? The fish is better."

"Anyway, Flama, why aren't you wearing your pressure suit?"

She poured a third drink. "I'm so fed up with it. It's uncomfortable and it messes up my clothes under it."

I felt my animosity starting to show. I poured myself another whiskey and then addressed her reluctance to wear the suit. "You know why we wear them, don't you? They stop oxygen bubbles from erupting in your bloodstream."

"I know that's what the instructions say, but we all take them off now and then. Toilet. Shower. Sex."

"Sex?" I knew that she was baiting me, but I continued. "The recommendation is that we don't have our suits off for more than an hour at a time except when sleeping and then no more than five hours."

She scoffed. "That's bunk, Hut. Pressure suits haven't been needed for decades. Sure, way back, people needed them, and they also needed helmets and oxygen tanks. They didn't even have artificial gravity. People just floated around. After a few months in space, bone density was diminished so that a return to Earth required months, if not years, of physical therapy."

Flama lectured me further. "These days, the atmospheric system in spacecraft, even a vessel as old as yours, is sufficient. We don't need a pressure suit. The reason we have them is that the pressure suit manufacturers' lobby has kept up the myth that they're a requirement, so the Council made it mandatory."

I had reached a point of being very fed up with Flama's cleverness. I knew she was probably right, but I resented her lauding her superiority over me again.

I shook my head. "The regulations say we wear them. So, we wear them. Understood?"

She gave me an odd look. "We can have them off for an hour at a time. Okay?"

The gin had loosened her up but she was not drunk. She knew exactly what she was doing.

She leered. "Sixty minutes should be enough. What do you think, space cadet?"

Her meaning was clear and I decided to humor her. "It takes me an hour to just get warmed up."

"I believe you just bragged."

Damn the woman. I rose and walked the three feet to stand in front of her, just a few inches away. I looked her full in the face. The perfume she was wearing wafted over me. Then, in line with legal guidance, I asked, "May I kiss you?"

Her blue eyes looked back at me and she gave a brief nod. Since every word spoken on board was recorded and the basis for any legal action, I said, "I need a verbal agreement to that. I'm not risking a charge or lawsuit."

"Okay, Captain, you may kiss me."

I leaned forward expecting that at any moment she would pull away and laugh at me. She started to do so, but I caught her and gave her a short peck on the lips and then I looked again into those amazing eyes, I said, "Fuck it" as I kissed her full on the lips for a long time. I felt the electric surge I had first experienced back on Canot40 pass through my body again. My mind recalled reading about this "love at first sight" reaction which can affect both men and women. But how could I be in love with this miserable woman? The voice recording system punctuated the air and caught my attention. "Hut Mur, you are fined $100 for that expletive."

Her arms wrapped around me, and I asked the logical follow-up question, to which she gave me an affirmative response. This dialog was also recorded.

A thought hit me. "You are protected, aren't you?"

"Hut, it's 2091. I've had birth control from the day I was born. Same procedure as stopping my mensural cycle. Can you imagine what women used to go through? Just the thought of a monthly period makes me feel ill."

She pouted a little and added, "And, no, I did not reverse my protection. We both know I could have done that but I didn't. You're safe." I motioned to my cabin and she nodded.

Years before, a sex worker on Saturn6 had schooled me well and I utilized all the skills and tricks she had taught me making love to Flama. I did not understand what initiated our actions since we clearly despised one another, but I found myself determined to provide her with an unforgettable experience. I knew I had succeeded when she cried out in, what I took to be, ecstasy, after thirty minutes or so.

I had not previously made love to a woman as beautiful as Flama Omm and I made the most of it.

Afterwards, I smiled but then a frown overtook my pleasure. How could someone so lovely be such a bitch?

We emerged from my cabin as Skrog entered the lounge. His six eyes took in the scene and his outer ones focused on the pair of us. He bubbled and left us to continue dressing.

Later that evening, Flama and I sat in the lounge. Neither of us seemed to have anything to say as we internalized what had just happened. "I'm going to bed," Flama announced, and I looked at her with anticipation. "On my own," she added. "By the way, Hut. The AirDryer in the shower is not working. It accepted my command but won't blow out any hot air."

"I have towels. You can use one of those."

"Gross!"

I shrugged. Our sex had been good. In fact, very good, but I now detected that she was having second thoughts and regretted what we had done.

"Are you okay?" I asked.

She looked blankly at me. "Fine. Just fine." Turning, she went to her cabin, closed the door after her, and I heard the magnetic lock engage.

TRANSCRIPT - WEC-47213-3492
World Power Grid Headquarters
Nuuk, Greenland

February 7, 2091/4:22 P.M.
Classification: Originally marked Personal - recoded Business

Grid Executive: NAME REDACTED, our scientists are sure that the new Delt is the solution, and piles of it, already refined, are sitting on Delta23. We need to get it shipped to Earth.

Aide: Awaiting your orders, sir.

Grid Executive: Track down a cargo vessel that can manage the operation and is close to the asteroid. Have them fly to it, load the Delt, and bring it here. Do it now.

Aide: Right away, sir.

PAUSE IN TRANSCRIPT

Aide: Excellent news, sir. There is a space tractor near the asteroid. It's old but it has ten cargo pods which will be more than sufficient. The pods are empty, so we won't even need to jettison any cargo. It should be easy.

Grid Executive: Good. Do it.

Aide: There is that legal issue and the ship's captain, a man named Hut Mur, might be a problem.

Grid Executive: How so?

Aide: He's not very smart. A CNARS. But he has a reputation for being opinionated and stubborn.

Grid Executive: I don't understand. Why does that make him a problem?

Aide: He might get some ideas about the Delt and its ownership.

Grid Executive: That would be unfortunate. Set up a meeting between me and Kul Lum. That'll be a personal discussion. No recordings.

On the morning of day eight, Flama sat opposite me for breakfast. Skrog had departed for the Control Center so we were alone. She looked at me and said, "Yesterday was a stupid mistake."

I smiled at her. "But it was rather good, though."

She snarled at me. "Don't you gloat, Hut Mur."

"I wasn't gloating. I was remarking on what happened."

"Bullshit,"

The voice recorder interrupted. "Flama Omm fined $100."

She glared at the speaker which had communicated her penalty.

She took a mouthful of cereal and, after swallowing it, said, "Anyway. It's not going to happen again. Perhaps I had too much to drink. An error I shall not make a second time." She drank her coffee and then consulted her wrist computer for the latest news reports.

That day, the strained relationship between Flama and me continued. She had not lost her determination to complain. On the other hand, she showed great affection for Skrog and laughed and joked with him.

Later, in the Control Center, I asked Skrog, "Why is she so nice to you and seems to despise me?"

He bubbled. "I am different species. Okay, she flirt with me. No possible sex. She like you lot. That scare her."

"You've got that wrong, Skrog. She doesn't like me at all."

"Skrog know these things, Cap."

That evening, before dinner, I was sitting in the lounge when Flama emerged from her cabin with wet hair and wearing only a towel.

"The shower water is not hot enough. Can you please fix it so I can finish washing my hair?"

I gazed at her. The towel was large but she was showing a lot of flesh and I found myself unable to concentrate on what she was saying.

"Stop looking at me, pervert."

I rolled my eyes and refocused. "That's odd. I have never had a problem with the water temperature. You did set the thermostat correctly, didn't you?"

"Of course, I did. Do I look stupid?"

I sighed. We were about to have another fight.

"Let me come and look." I followed her into her cabin and through to the bathroom. The shower thermostat indicated that it was set to 38 degrees, more than hot enough.

"The setting is correct. I don't understand." The bathroom was small and she was standing close to me. I smelt the perfume in her hair from the gel shampoo that she had applied before turning on the shower. It was floral, and I felt her warmth as we stood face-to-face at the narrow entrance. But I turned away from her and again looked at the setting.

"You used a voice command to set the temperature. Right?"

"Of course."

Then I noticed what had caused the problem. "Did it ask whether you wanted Celsius or Fahrenheit?"

"I don't recall. Why?"

I spoke to the shower. "Shower Command." It flashed its blue light. At least one voice-based system can understand me. "What temperature are you showing? The response came. "Temperature set at 38 degrees Fahrenheit."

"Reset to 38 degrees Celsius."

"Done."

"Shower command. Turn on the shower."

The shower started.

I said, "Try it now, Flama."

She reached over and held her hand under the cascading water. Her expression indicated she understood the mistake she had made and she gave me a weak smile.

"It's fine now. Thanks, Hut. That was stupid of me. I'm a scientist, so of course I know the difference between Celsius and Fahrenheit."

We were still standing close together in the doorway to the bathroom and as she turned to face me, the towel she had pulled around her, slipped. It fell to the floor.

I should have just picked it up, handed it to her, and left. But the sight of her magnificent naked body caused me to stand still and look at her.

She appeared shocked, used her hands and arms to try and cover her nakedness, and reddened. She looked at me without saying anything for what seemed an eternity. Her arms dropped away and I could see all of her loveliness. She did not ask my permission but put her arms around me and kissed me.

I heard my voice saying, "Shower command, water off."

The first time that we had sex together had been a frantic one, with each of us succumbing to animal lust as I applied everything that my teacher on Saturn6 had taught me. The result had been one of ecstasy but without any feeling.

This time was different. Each of us showed tenderness, and we spent a long time pleasing one another.

We finally fell asleep in each other's arms. Neither of us ate dinner that night.

Chapter Eight

Three days later, we arrived in our Jupiter orbit, and the dynamics on board had changed over that time. Flama and I had tempted fate and spent significant time not wearing our pressure suits, but we were suffering no ill effects.

When we started the eleven-day trip there had been a conflict between us that grew to a point where I was dreaming up ways to kill her and dispose of the body in space. She still owed me the second part of her payment for passage, and I imagined removing her left hand and scanning it but, I knew that the chip automatically deactivated if life signs were missing, so that would not work. Perhaps it would be worth it even if I sacrificed the payment.

But the sex we enjoyed after the shower episode changed everything. It was different than the first time and far more enjoyable. It was no longer a competition. Each of us seemed to want to please the other and we could not get enough. I would signal to her or she would signal to me and we would repair to my cabin, or sometimes, for variety, hers. Skrog sat back and rolled all six eyes at the same time and bubbled.

Two nights before we arrived at Jupiter, Flama was sleeping with me in my cabin, and at about 2:00 AM, I was sound asleep when I felt her shaking my shoulder. For the record, I am a heavy sleeper and hate being woken. "Not now, darling, Flama."

The shaking continued and I heard her voice continue, "Hut, wake up. I want to talk."

"I'm asleep. Let's talk in the morning."

"I can't sleep. I have something important on my mind.'

I was starting to become annoyed. "It'll keep till the morning."

"No, it won't."

I realized that there was nothing I could do to have her wait until a reasonable hour, so I wiped my eyes and sat up in bed. "Okay. What's so urgent?"

Her eyes gleamed in the half-darkness of my cabin and I saw that she too sat upright, looking at me. "Hut, what is your ambition? You have a space tractor now but you can't just want to stay on this ship for the rest of your life. Do you want to build a company with several tractors maybe even dozens of them and people working for you?"

She exhaled. "Or is the tractor just an interim move before going back to Earth and starting something new?"

I was still groggy from being woken and there did not seem to be an urgent aspect of her questioning, so I rolled over and tried to go back to sleep. I think a small snore may have escaped me and Flama suddenly pounded on my back. "Wake up, you bastard." I did not. I returned to a sound sleep.

The next day, Day 10, Flama seemed rather frosty and I vaguely remembered our conversation early that morning. She did not raise the matter, so I ignored it without realizing the importance of what she had asked me.

That night we shifted our sleeping arrangements to her bed and after a satisfying encounter, I drifted off into a happy sleep. I am not sure what time it happened but it was probably about 3:00 AM when she shook me from my slumber, as she had done the previous night, and said, "Hut, I'm confused."

Oh, God. What now?

"About what?"

"About Skrog's English."

"What about it?" I did not need this.

"The Martians are technologically advanced, yet Skrog still speaks broken English. You can buy a perfect translation implant module for every language on Earth. It interfaces with your wrist computer and enables you to speak and understand fluent French, Russian, Chinese, whatever."

I let out a breath which should have told her that I was still groggy and not interested in discussing Skrog's English.

Her eyes shone brightly and I knew I had to rouse myself and discuss this trivial, non-urgent matter. "You're right. But what does that have to do with Skrog?"

She gave me an exasperated look. "His English isn't perfect."

"I know that. But I can always understand what he means. Can't you?"

"Yes. But why can't he speak English fluently?"

By now, I had become fully awake and smiled in the semi-darkness of her cabin. "Having observed this years ago, one night after Skrog and I had consumed several Galactics, I raised that question with him."

Flama seemed interested in the answer, but I contemplated stringing her out with some half answers to watch her get more and more frustrated. That would have been a childish act on my part, so I correctly abandoned the urge and gave her the explanation. I also wanted to finish this conversation and get back to sleep.

"Back in 2049, when the Martians first met with Earth's leaders and made their deal, swapping their technology for land on Earth, they used one of their technologies which allowed them to translate their own language and speech profiles into something that the Earth presidents could understand."

She nodded. "Okay. I can see that this would be an acceptable short-term solution but…"

I continued, "Following that, a working party of linguists from Mars and a mirror group from Earth was set up. Over the years, people on Earth have learned languages from people who spoke two or more. There are many common roots and each language is structured in a fairly similar manner."

Flama nodded again, and I said, "The 'Martian' language, as you heard when Skrog named his original home world, has a wider range of sounds and harmonics with grunts and songs punctuating the dialog."

I had her attention. "The linguists from Earth couldn't understand any part of the Martian language and had no basis for translating it. The same was true for the Martian linguists. They ended up with a translator module which only provided a subset of the languages. With the Martian population being only about one hundred thousand and them living away from humans on Mars, the need for something better was never seen as a priority. Martians continued to speak to each other in their native language and Earthlings adopted English as the global norm. No company or government saw the requirement for anything other than the rudimentary translations back in 2049."

Flama reached out and stroked my arm, and I concluded, "Maybe, with the Martians moving to Earth, they'll address the issue."

She shook her head. "When, or maybe if, they move to Earth they'll end up in some remote area and, I believe, they'll be cut off from their Earthling neighbors."

I had to agree with her.

She smiled and kissed me. "You know a lot, Hut."

"I have always been curious about how things work. I don't always know the details but I'm good at the high-altitude stuff."

She had snuggled up to me and I saw that she had fallen asleep, while I was now completely awake. I could not help thinking about this woman and our relationship. When she flew down to Jupiter the next day, I would be rid of an irritating person but something told me that I would miss her.

I looked over at her and sighed. My experience with women was minimal. I left home at age eighteen and spent all my life in space, where there were no female relationships. Well, there were some since each of the truck stops and colonial outposts had its share of hookers. But they were not young and not beautiful and their services were for sale. Over the years, I have taken vacations on Earth and dated a few women. But besides some one-night stands, my experience was limited and included no long-term relationships.

My mind traveled back to the older sex worker on Saturn6 station many years before. She seemed to like me and took me under her wing. When we first met, she looked me up and down and asked. "Virgin?"

I lied. "Of course not."

I had my name printed on my overalls and she read it. "Hut Mur, I'm going to teach you all you need to know to make a woman very happy."

As TESVG will attest, I am a quick learner and methodical. The woman on Saturn6 taught me the skills that I brought to my relationship with Flama, but I improvised a few twists of my own. I believe that Tes would have awarded me an A plus.

However, the woman on Saturn6 did not teach me that a relationship between two humans can go beyond sex. She did not mention that there could be something outside physical enjoyment. I thought about my feelings for Flama. They seemed to make that transition, but without previous experience, I wasn't sure. In many of the fictional videos I watched, there was often what the actors called "love." Was I falling in love?

On several occasions over the past few days, she appeared about to tell me something and then pulled back. My insecurities cut in. Probably she thought I was not good enough, or smart enough, for her. I decided to ask her the question which was uppermost on my mind.

The next morning, over breakfast, I said, "Where do we go from here, Flama?"

She shrugged. "I leave the ship, shuttle across to Jupiter Station and you sail off into space to Saturn."

"You know what I mean." I laid my hand on her arm.

Skrog had been sitting with us and now rose, "I go check engine." He left us.

I made a decision, perhaps impetuously. "You could stay on board and come to Saturn. I could drop you back here on my way to Mars. Your Jupiter herbs will still be here if you don't get to them for another month or so." She dropped her head to the right. It was a little motion which I had noticed lately and I found it endearing. It implied that she was giving something serious thought.

However, one thing missing from our relationship was knowing more about her. I knew about her job but I had not been able to coax her to tell me more about her family and upbringing. The fact that she had few real friends, if any, was concerning. We couldn't just have sex 24/7 for the rest of our lives. Or maybe we could. The pharmaceuticals available today are wicked. I decided to address the issue, but without realizing it, my face adopted a serious expression.

She did not smile but said "You have something you want to talk about. Yes?"

I sighed. "True." She had come to know me well despite our short history.

Looking at her directly, I said, "I think I may have feelings about you."

"I should hope you would."

"Beyond sex."

"Oh."

"But a few things are worrying me."

"For instance?"

"Your background. Everything you've told me starts with your graduation from TESVG. You're very smart, and that's okay by me."

I tried to remember the lessons that Tes had taught me about empathy and how to ask awkward questions in a way that does not offend.

I started with "Tell me about your upbringing. Your parents, siblings, friends?"

She winced and sat down on the lounge seat and curled her feet up under her. "That's something I've put behind me. Please don't push me to tell you."

I grunted.

"Damn it." She said the words quietly and then added, "If it wasn't early morning, I'd request a gin."

"How about a coffee?"

"Sure."

I ordered one from the Uni-cooker and handed it to her. She sipped the strong, dark brew.

Tes's instructions came back to me from a social skills course eight years before. "Remain silent and the person you are talking to will feel the need to talk." I looked at Flama without speaking.

"You're pulling Lesson 342.21 on me, aren't you?" She gave a short, bitter laugh. "I took the same course. 'Remain silent…' wasn't it?"

I laughed as well and kissed her. At first, she did not respond and looked away. Then she turned to me and spoke. "Okay. Buckle your seat harness." She put down the coffee and ordered a glass of chilled water from the dispenser.

Chapter Nine

Flama gulped the water, and I expected her to complain about the sour taste. She did not, but she started her story: "I was born in Hollywood on the North American West Coast. My father was a senior executive in the video industry, and we lived in a mansion with swimming pools and extensive grounds. My mother was a socialite, spending most of her time on committees for the poor and disadvantaged." I took the last comment as a sarcastic rebuke.

"My parents were loving and devoted to bringing up my brother and me. We were spoiled. We had platinum, implanted chips at birth, and enrolled in the Diamond version of TESVG. Our vacations were to the best resorts and we even once took a one-month trip on a private Speeder to the new complex in Ganymede.

She had my attention and I asked, "Who was your father? Have I heard of him?"

"I'm not going to identify him. You'll see why later in the story. My second name, Omm, is not my born name. I changed it."

This was getting interesting. "What did your dad do?"

"He was a technologist. He ran the team that developed the APVC."

I had not heard of this. "What's that?"

"It's an AI system for creating videos. Actors go through a profiling step that captures everything about them in holographics. How they stand, walk, run, jump, sit. How they look serious, laugh, cry, show pain, show happiness. All the things that distinguish them. The actor signs a contract with one of the studios and spends a week or so developing their profile. That's all they have to do. Then, when the studio decides to launch a new movie, the producer keys in a few notes on the plot and names the actors. Minutes later, the completed holographic video is created and can be downloaded to home screens or mega-theaters. No one can tell the difference between this and a movie filmed on a set using the real actors."

This was incredible. "Why would someone agree to that?"

"Money – World Dollars. The artist negotiates an up-front payment to permit the development and storage of his or her profile. They negotiate their rights regarding videos made by the studios. Most have a right to review each production and, if they don't like it or think they are endangering their brand, reject it or demand changes. The actors are paid based on the success of the movies, and advertisements. After the profiling step, they sit back and cash in without lifting a finger. Even interviews on the late shows are generated by the profile while the actor sits at home watching, drinking, or taking designer drugs."

She walked over to the counter and replenished her glass of water. "My dad also added an interactive capability so the viewer can decide the mood of the movie – sad or happy – and even the outcome – the hero lives or dies. He developed the technology mid-century but it took another ten years or so to convince the actors and their agents to sign on to this new approach."

This was heavy stuff and I smiled. "So that's how I can view Mission Impossible #372 starring Tom Cruise. It was just released, and we both know that Tom died over fifty years ago." I continued, "So if your dad masterminded that technology, he must have been in high demand and very rich."

"He was …" her voice trailed off.

"You must have been a happy family."

"We were but then the excrement hit the fan." Her choice of words tricked the voice recorder which remained silent.

I waited for her to continue.

"I was nineteen at the time and was engrossed in my studies when there was a chime from the entrance and when our service robot answered it, I saw a group of armed marshals the leader of whom announced that he held a warrant for my father's arrest. Dad was furious but they restrained him and took him away to their station."

"What was the charge?"

"I didn't find out until later. My mom told me."

She sipped her water. "Mom was even angrier than my father and swore that the guilty party was Sus Pagu, who was the corporation's CEO. "

Flama had still not told me the crime that her father had been accused of. I looked at her and raised my eyebrows.

"The charge, Mom said, was that Dad had copied the software and most of the actor profiles and sold them to a Vietnamese pornography site. They used the system and the profiles to create and distribute porn videos featuring North America's best and brightest actors. Deep fake on steroids. The authorities said this was a major felony."

"I can see that."

She continued, "I was young and very headstrong at the time." I could not help rolling my eyes. "I insisted on attending the virtual trial which took place within the mandatory one-month timeline from indictment."

"He pleaded not guilty?"

"That's where it gets weird. He did but he put up little defense. His AI attorney attempted to have him explain a series of communications that implicated him. It was a smart bot, and it made the point that the evidence was just too neat. And no one could show how Dad benefited. Global financial searches showed no flow of funds from the Vietnamese to him."

She drank a small amount of the water she had been nursing. "The jury system had been replaced by the current AI deliberation approach so the verdict came in within a few minutes."

"So what did the jurist bot find?

"Guilty."

This sank in.

"Appeals?"

"Dad refused to appeal."

"Did you talk with him? Did he do it?"

"We had some holo-calls but he was always evasive. He seemed to want to avoid the subject and it made me think that he was probably guilty."

She put her water down and reached over to the coffee she had left on the counter. She drank all that remained in the cup. "Mom was devastated. What she called 'Dad's disgrace' caused all her friends to desert her. And then we found out that our homes were mortgaged and when our income stopped abruptly, the lending companies foreclosed."

I offered her a fresh coffee and she nodded.

"A year before, the World Court had passed the Individual's Right to Terminate ruling, allowing any adult to end their life for any reason and Mom took advantage of that. My brother was a year older than me and decided to join her. A few days later, I was informed that, when my father heard the news, he screamed in torment and shortly afterward insisted that he too, be allowed to suicide. I was twenty-one years of age, alone and penniless."

My heart went out to her and I started to understand her bitterness. "So, what did you do?"

"Some family friends reached out and took me in. They were great but I lived with my demons. I hated the world and the people in it and threw myself into my studies with TESVG. I projected my feelings into a contentious relationship with Tes. Yes, I called my TESVG interface

"Tes" just as you told me you did. She pushed me hard and it was a fight all the way. She drove me to always insist on winning and never to quit. I graduated with a high A in the top one percent and started my work as a biologist in space."

Flama's interaction with the learning system was different from mine. My interface with Tes was a lot less aggressive, and I realized that Tes had adapted to Flama's personality. I said, "Understood," but I wasn't sure I did. Following up, I said, "I can see now why you have had few real friends or relationships."

She stopped speaking and was obviously thinking through what she would say next.

Then she said, "Actually, I had a lot of relationships with guys. And that is the problem. Early on I created a checklist of what I wanted in a partner. One of the primary criteria was that he was ambitious and rich. I have always had relationships with wealthy men and have never gone into one without having an exit plan. Whenever it started to get serious, I bailed. And it's always been me who instigated the break-up, not the guy. I vowed I would never end up being hurt. Every time, the guy has been gutted and I breezed out. I'm not a nice person, Hut."

I did not speak but my mind was racing. Her story explained a lot and I felt sorry for her but I also reflected, will I be the next of the pile of male bodies in her wake?

But, since she had only ever been interested in ambitious and wealthy men, a relationship with me was unlikely to happen.

She stood, paced about the lounge, and then looked me straight in the eyes. "It's probably a stupid idea but staying on board and taking the trip with you to Saturn sounds good. I've always wanted to see how you harvest tons of ice and load it into cargo pods. That's if the offer is still open."

I paused but gave her a guarded grin, embraced her, and muttered "Sure." Skrog had just rejoined us and, overhearing her request and my reply, bubbled.

We decoupled from our mooring buoy and were about to set out for Saturn when a message came through from Earth. It requested a holo-call and five minutes later, I sat in my Control Center projecting my likeness into the system. I had an odd premonition about the call and decided to delay our departure until after I had taken it. My ship has personal holo-call setups throughout the vessel but for serious work, I used the enhanced version in the Control Center and I took the call there.

Another image entered the holograph. He was a tall, cleanly-shaven man dressed in expensive, fashionable attire. "Hello. I am Kul Lum. I'm calling from Earth and I have a contract that we want you to implement for us."

"Hello, Kul. I'm Hut Mur. Pleased to meet you." The social skills modules of my TESVG training sprang into my mind. "How can I help you?"

"We have an urgent need for a cargo to be collected from a body in the Asteroid Belt and transported to Earth."

"Who is the customer?"

The image paused and it was clear, that Kul Lum did not want to reveal his employer.

"It's not necessary that you know that."

I countered, "There is. The World Council has strict rules about the responsibilities of space haulage companies. It's to police transportation of illegal goods - drugs, some metals, armaments. They insist that the company requesting the shipping is identified."

There was a pause and Kul Lum uttered a sigh. "Well, Hut, can't we bypass that?"

"No way. I would lose my license, and that is not acceptable."

Lum nodded slowly and then said, "It's World Energy Corporation."

I smiled. This was a reputable entity that I knew was the largest corporation on Earth.

"Sounds interesting. I have a current project I'm just starting. I need to take a run to Saturn and then back to Mars. We'll be transporting ice and the loading and unloading adds a few weeks to the trip. Let me check the timing." I entered some data into my wrist computer. "Okay. I can start your job in two months."

A useful feature of the commercial version of the holo-call is that the entirety of every participant's body language is visible and I noticed Kul's left foot beating away when I mentioned the timescale.

It was clear that he found the timing unacceptable. But he stayed calm and said, "Gosh, Hut. That's a long time. How can we shorten it? Perhaps you can postpone your current job and do this one for me first." He gave me a smirk that told me that he was used to having his way in contractual matters. He looked away and flicked a speck of lint from the arm of his cashmere jacket.

I was starting to dislike this man. "Sorry, but I have a current contract that I need to honor. My customer has already paid me half the fee." Well, would do so in a few weeks.

Kul's smile disappeared. "I'll make it worth your while. I'll pay them back their up-front payment. No harm's done. But I need you to start immediately."

"Kul, I'll say this again. I will not break a contract. I have a reputation to uphold."

"How about…" He named an outlandish amount of money.

Flama had joined Skrog and me in the Control Center but stood back from the holo-call. They signaled to me and I muted the call. Flama said, "That fee seems very high."

I replied, "Yes. And we still don't know what he wants us to do. It sounds like something illegal. Or maybe, multiple shipments."

I unmuted the call. "Well, Kul, tell me more about what you want."

"I want to tell you that personally."

It was obvious that Kul wanted to keep our discussion secret and that is difficult in a holo-call where the voice recording system analyzed the conversation and was good at detecting impropriety.

He continued, "I'll fly up to you."

"From Earth? You'll fly up here to Jupiter?"

"Yes."

"That's over seven hundred million kilometers. That's quite a trip just for a meeting."

"This is an important contract and I want to brief you face-to-face. I have your coordinates. Stay where you are and I'll be with you in ten days. I'll transfer the first payment, 50%, into escrow before I leave and I want you to delay your current job. Can you do that?"

I thought about it. The ice contract was agreed at a basic fee rate for the shipment, which was one-hundredth of what Kul was offering. Kul's payment would allow me to pay off the remaining loan on my tractor in full and my customer for the ice had indicated that he was in no hurry. Pushing it off by a month or two would not impact our relationship. "Okay. That shouldn't be a problem."

I gave him my legal escrow account details and terminated the call. Flama looked at me. "That is a shitload of money, Hut. Let's hope it doesn't come with a shitload of trouble for you." Then she added, "I wonder what he wants us to do."

The voice recorder system joined the conversation. "Two expletives. Flama Omm, you are fined $200."

Since it would take about ten days for Kul Lum to reach us, I said to Flama, "While we're waiting, do you want to check out your herb project?"

"Good idea. Can you shuttle me over to the station?"

Chapter Ten

TRANSCRIPT - WCS-61479-52176
World Council - Security Branch
Singapore
February 12, 2091/1:12 P.M.
Classification: Originally marked Personal - recoded Government

All participants were joined by holo-call.

Inspector General: The meeting will come to order. Roll call.

PAUSE

Inspector General: States of North America

Delegate 1: Present

Inspector General: States of Central and South America

Delegate 2: Present

Inspector General: States of Europe

Delegate 3: Present

Inspector General: States of Africa

Delegate 4: Present

Inspector General: States of Asia/Australia

Delegate 5: Present

Inspector General: Consortium of Other Countries

Delegate 6: Present

Inspector General: Let the record show all countries of Earth are represented.

PAUSE

Inspector General: Item number one is classified as "Top Secret." The Energy Crisis. Inspector of Issues, please report.

Inspector of Issues: Gentlemen and ladies, as you all know, we have a predicament on our hands. The World Power Grid is on the point of failing. Fortunately, other than the first German outage, the Grid has worked impeccably.

Inspector General: Are you saying we don't have a problem?

Inspector of Issues: Oh, there's definitely a problem. Grid management has it contained and the network has held up. But over time, as more and more batteries stop operating, we will certainly have a problem. A catastrophe.

Inspector General: How bad?

Inspector of Issues: If all the batteries fail, we shall not be able to provide power other than when the sun shines or the wind blows. There will be power outages all over the world. We don't have backup generators like they did early in the century and are wholly reliant on batteries. Hospitals will be without power, The world economy will crash like we've never experienced before. In winter, millions of people will freeze to death. Everything is driven by electricity. Since the end of the War and the transition to a world-based orientation, we've seen a period of peace and economically stable growth. Failure of the Grid will destroy that.

Inspector General: How long do we have?

Inspector of Issues: World Energy Corporation, which operates the Grid, estimates about five months.

Delegate 3: In Europe, particularly the Kingdom, there are already problematic signs. When they dropped the "United" from its title and voted to rejoin their sister countries on the continent, they did not invest in the superconducting backbone that was recommended.

Instead, they chose to rely more heavily on local battery clusters. That was back in 2066 and they have not upgraded since. That wasn't a problem when the batteries worked but now the threat is real. So far, their part of the network is holding, but this area will likely be one of the first to crash. This is a very vulnerable situation.

Inspector General: Has World Energy found a solution yet?

Inspector of Issues: Yes. The electrodes, which are based on the Delt metal, are becoming depleted and this is the cause of the issue. World Energy believes the solution is to swap out the depleted metal with new, unused components. Their tests show that this will work.

Inspector General: How do we get this Delt? I thought it was only found on that asteroid, Delta23.

Inspector of Issues: That's true, sir, but fortunately, a large quantity of the refined metal is still there. It's sitting on the asteroid. We just need to scoop it up, ship it to Earth, and change out the components.

Inspector General: Are steps in place to do that?

Inspector of Issues: Yes. World Energy is commissioning a space tractor to pick up the metal.

Inspector General: Can they get it here in time?

Inspector of Issues: They believe so. The time it will take for the freighter to reach Delta23, load the Delt, ship it here, and for World Energy to swap out the current batteries is within the timescale they estimate for the Grid to fail. Providing nothing goes wrong, we should be fine.

Inspector General: Let's hope so.

I directed my tractor's forward cameras to take in the vastness of Jupiter and its satellite moons. Scientists call Jupiter a gas giant since it is over 1,000 times the volume of Earth but has just 300 times the mass of my home world. Regardless, it's a large planet. Its surface has an atmosphere that is 90% hydrogen and it rotates rapidly – a day here lasts less than eleven Earth hours.

I knew the scientific community had made attempts to access the planet's resources, but these had been confined to agricultural experiments that had enjoyed limited success. The humans managing the projects lived off the planet on a station in space with an orbit matching Jupiter's largest moon, Ganymede.

The Jupiter space station is one million kilometers from the planet's surface and provides the headquarters for the Jupiter Scientific Study team. It was with this group that Flama was to work on her low-light herb assignment.

Flama consulted her wrist computer and found the man in charge of her project. She made a call using the commercial-grade holo-call system in the Control Center, and I listened to her conversation.

"Hello, my name is Flama Omm, and I work for TESVG. I sent you my credentials several weeks ago together with an outline of my mission. Are you the right person to be talking to?"

The scientist's holograph showed a short man, probably in his seventies, dressed in a white jacket that appeared to have been recently washed and ironed. His gray beard was well-trimmed, and his deportment and mannerisms made it clear to me that this man had an ego the size of an endangered elephant.

He spoke with a northern European accent. Swedish?

"Hello, Ms. Omm. Yes, I received your credentials. Impressive. But I am afraid that you have wasted your time. My agricultural team has been singularly unsuccessful in growing these herbs. Some existed when we arrived here ten years ago but since then they have suffered from some disease and only a few remain. And they are unhealthy. Your trip has been in vain."

"I don't understand. TESVG reviewed all the research before commissioning me to come out here. This is an expensive project for them. I find it hard to believe that they got it wrong."

The scientist's body language indicated that he was angry at what Flama had just told him.

"Unfortunately, they were mistaken. The herbs are worthless and you have no role to play out here. I suggest you return to Earth and choose another path for your career."

Flama was aghast, an emotion that quickly turned to anger. "I shall have to check with my manager." She signaled for Skrog to terminate the call.

She stood, still processing what the scientist had just told her and I asked, "Do you believe him?"

She turned to me. "Why would he lie?"

"Let me try something." I had a few friends on Jupiter Station from previous trips there and one worked in the Scientific Study group. I called him.

"I'm hoping you can help me with something."

"After you saved me in that bar brawl a year back, I owe you, Hut. Anything I can do, I will."

"The head of the department there. A Swedish-sounding man. Do you know him?"

"Oh yes. Leif Eric. If you want me to describe him, you'll need to pay several hundred World Dollars for the swear words that I'll use."

"Can you be more specific?"

"Arrogant, narcissistic, self-centered, and ruthless. Everyone hates him and he's not even a good scientist. The only success he's achieved is in developing a breed of herbs which can grow in Jupiter's hydrogen-based atmosphere."

Flama was listening and nearly screamed with rage.

I continued the call. "He just told a colleague of mine, that the herb project had been unsuccessful. That seems to be a lie."

"Well, Hut. There is a rumor that Mr. Eric has secured a contract with a food company on Earth for distribution of the herbs."

Flama interjected, "The charter of the Study group prohibits that. He's breaking his agreement with the sponsors."

"That may be but the rumor has been around for several months and I know that he has shipped a significant volume of something back to Earth. One of my admin people handles shipping."

We spoke for a few more minutes, and I thanked him and ended the call.

"That slimebucket." Flama's description did not trigger a fine from the voice recorder.

I asked her, "What do you want to do?"

She shook her head. "I need to think this through. Challenging him will make working with him a nightmare. Blowing a whistle on him will generate a mountain of paperwork, depositions, and involvement of lawyer bots."

I decided to change the subject. "Jupiter Station is in the same orbit as Ganymede. You mentioned that you visited the resort there when you were young. Feel like going back. It's fairly close and we could have a few days while you think through what you want to do about Leif Eric."

The frown on her face changed to a broad smile. "And we can get off this claustrophobic tractor."

Ganymede is Jupiter's largest moon. Just as Jupiter dwarfs all the other planets in the Solar System, it is the largest moon in the System, being only 2.4 times smaller than Earth. Like Earth's moon, it is tidally locked to Jupiter, such that the same area on the surface faces the planet throughout its seven-earth-day planetary orbit.

The Z-Resort was to receive the tons of water that I would bring from Saturn, and I had visited it on three other occasions. Built in 2075, it was located on the Jupiter-facing side so the guests could enjoy a constant view of the large planet. However, as Ganymede makes its seven-day orbit, the resort is bathed in darkness for about half of that time.

When I moored my tractor and its pods, Flama, Skrog and I took the shore boat and drove down to the resort. The cameras showed the impressive structure.

A huge, transparent dome covering 200 square kilometers enclosed a series of buildings which I knew to be hotels, restaurants, sporting facilities, museums, art galleries, administrative offices, and staff and robot housing. There were also a hundred or so luxury villas and five swimming pools.

Flama had changed into what she described as resort wear: a pair of white shorts and knee-high boots (also in white), a bright green bikini top, and a lighter green coverall in Indian cotton. I wore my overalls, as these were the only clothing I owned.

After landing and tethering my craft, we proceeded through the airlock which attached itself to our shuttle, and entered the resort. Skrog excused himself and set off to a bar that he knew was frequented by fellow Martians.

A robot, dressed in what I now knew was resort wear, welcomed us.

Flama asked the bot, "We need a men's clothing boutique."

I glared at her. "What for? I'm not buying some expensive clothes that I'll never wear again."

"Oh yes, you are, Hut Mur. With the Kul Lum contract, you'll have a bunch of World Dollars that you'll never be able to spend in space."

"But I can invest them. That's what I've been doing for the past fifteen years and I have amassed a tidy sum. Even without Lum's job, I shall be able to pay off the loan on my tractor within…"

She scoffed. "Okay. I'll buy you the clothes. I'm not going to walk around the resort and go to a nice restaurant with someone dressed in old overalls."

An hour later, I wore a blue linen mid-sleeve shirt in the collarless, modern style over matching dark blue shorts. Flama had also insisted I purchase some espadrilles, in a light blue. Somehow, I ended up paying.

The temperature under the dome was constant at 27 degrees Celsius, and I knew that the sunlight would last another two days before the artificial sun lights were turned on for the next three or four days of darkness.

Flama selected a restaurant for lunch and we settled into what was designed as an Italian trattoria with genuine, imported, wooden tables and chairs. The walls were paneled in rough wood. Classic dishes were offered and most seemed to be real rather than synthetic. The wine, said to be from Umbria, complemented the meal and I enjoyed the change of venue from the tractor and the quality and variety of the food. But it was expensive!

Flama was ecstatic. "So much better than grilled chicken." I nodded my agreement as she added, "And I can swing my arms and not hit a wall."

"Feel like a game after lunch?"

Flama looked up, "What sort of game?"

"Halfgrav pickleball."

She looked at me curiously. "I've heard of pickleball, but what is this halfgrav thing?"

"The court has a separate artificial gravity system and they turn it off for games. With Ganymede's mass being about half that of Earth, you play at a half level of gravity. It's easy to jump ten or twelve feet in the air. It's fun."

"I've never played sports. There doesn't seem a point to them."

"Want to try?"

An hour later, we were on the court and shortly afterward I could see that sport and Flama did not go together.

She threw down her paddle as she bounced across the court. "This is a stupid game. Is there anyone else you can play with?"

I accessed my wrist computer, found a player of about my standard, and within a few minutes was leaping up and down and sending the ball rocketing. We played two games as Flama watched and shouted her encouragement. My opponent played well but I won each of the games.

Flama appeared to enjoy observing the play but I was aware that she was becoming bored. I stopped the game and asked. "Feel like a swim?"

We walked to one of the swimming pools and she changed into a small bikini before plunging into the blue water. "Hut, you should have bought a swimsuit."

"No point. I can't swim."

"Really?"

"Growing up, my family didn't have a pool and we never visited a resort with one. When I started work, it was in space, and there were only pools at a few stations throughout the solar system.

I watched her enjoy herself. She laughed and sang a little song but I knew that sooner or later, she would remember that she had to return to my tractor and that moment would be difficult for her.

I made a decision. "Let's stay here overnight."

"Really? That would be so nice."

I called Skrog and he was pleased to spend the night on Ganymede. "I stay with friend here."

I booked a double room for Flama and me, in the main complex, a Z-hotel. She kissed me lightly on the lips and said, "You'll need some more clothes to go to dinner, tonight."

That night, we ate at a high-end French establishment, Le Gavroche, which had been styled after a famous turn-of-the-century restaurant in London. The waiter bots were dressed in formal attire, with black trousers, white dinner jackets, and black bowties. The tables were covered in starched tablecloths and arrayed with the finest flatware, as well as crystal glassware. The menu was classical French and the sommelier bot recommended some excellent wines to accompany each of the courses.

"What do you think, Hut?"

"I like it." I meant this sentiment but knew at the end of the meal, I would be facing a serious bill. Previously, in other high-end establishments that I rarely visited, the mounting cost had always spoiled my enjoyment, but this night was special. I put money out of my mind and relaxed in the company of this attractive woman.

Flama seemed at home in the restaurant as she debated the menu with the waiter bot and the sommelier.

"What are you going to eat?" she asked me.

I looked at the menu, which was printed on paper in a heavy leather binder in the traditional style. It was in French, a language I did not know at all. "I have no idea," I said.

"They have a filet of lamb which was flown up from Earth and are serving it with a mustard sauce."

"Sounds good to me."

She pointed to one item. "Look they have *poulet grille*."

I smiled. My limited French did extend to knowing grilled chicken when I saw it.

Through the meal, Flama was a different woman. She laughed and chatted about herself and a couple of friends, and she sprinkled in some anecdotes regarding her relationship with Tes and some of the vacations she took as a young girl.

I was feeling in a good mood as well and told her stories about the various ports of call in the System.

We talked for two hours as the multitude of courses were delivered and consumed.

I thoroughly enjoyed the experience and she appeared to do so as well.

"I couldn't do this every night, but now and then it's such fun."

We completed the evening with coffee that was far better than I had on the tractor, and I was about to request the bill when a man, dressed formally in a suit, approached our table.

He looked directly at me. "Hut Mur, isn't it?"

"Yes."

"I'm Bej Slon. I'm the CEO of the resort and wanted to welcome you back, Mr. Mur."

I did not know him but had dealt with his team on a few occasions.

He stood there and I motioned for him to join us. A robo-waiter brought over a chair and the man lowered himself into it.

I had risen to greet him and now gestured to Flama. "Mr. Slon, this is my companion, Flama Omm."

He took her hand and kissed it. Smooth bastard.

"Did you enjoy your dinner tonight?"

She gave him her best smile and said, "Oh yes. It was splendid."

He spoke to her, "Your Mr. Mur has performed some valuable services for the resort. His contracts have always been for delivery of water or other goods but he has always gone beyond his brief and provided additional value. On one occasion, one of our water holding tanks sprang a leak and he sacrificed a contract he was operating to fly to Mars and bring back specialized equipment that we needed to repair it."

She looked at me but I could not read her expression. Was she favorably impressed?

Slon engaged in a short conversation, showing his skills in small talk. He said, "Thank you for joining us tonight, and I thank you for your helpful deeds over the years. I shall pick up the bill—restaurant, and hotel room." He added, "By the way, I upgraded you to a suite."

I cursed myself for not ordering a high-end cognac. But the meal had been exceptional and would not deplete my credit balance by a single World Dollar.

The restaurant was located a few kilometers from the hotel, so I called a robo-taxi, and ten minutes later, we checked in. I scanned my implant and the system recognized my details and directed me to a suite on the penthouse floor.

The accommodation comprised a large living area, including a well-stocked bar, a bathroom, and a bedroom with a round bed in the center. I communicated my Earth time zone; the room prepared lighting to reflect that. Above the bed, the ceiling was a room-wide screen simulating the stars that we would have seen if we were open to the sky.

I poured a champagne for Flama and a cognac for myself, as she jumped up and down on the bed. She smiled at me and said, "Thanks for a lovely day, Hut. Now I want you to make love to me."

Chapter Eleven

We checked out the next morning and returned to the tractor. Within a few hours, we were mooring near Jupiter Station.

As we sat in the lounge, still wearing our resort wear, she reached out to me. "Darling, that was so much fun. I haven't laughed like that for years. And the food was terrific. Thanks for putting up with me and giving me such a great time." She kissed me long and hard.

My thoughts mirrored hers. It was the best couple of days of my life. But even with Bej Slon's generosity, the clothes had cost a fortune!

I asked her, "Have you decided what to do about Leif Eric?"

She shook her head. She had forgotten about it while we were on Ganymede and was still unsure how to handle the matter.

She winced. "I still haven't decided what to do. We have no proof that he's up to no good, but I can't just allow him to get away with it."

"Let me try something."

She adopted an aggressive stance. "What are you going to do?"

"If I told you, I'd have to kill you."

"You are such an idiot, Hut."

"So, do you want me to help?"

"Alright. But this had better work."

She returned to her cabin and, I heard her say, out loud, "This cabin is so small."

An hour later, Skrog knocked on her door and told her that Leif Eric was on a holo-call and wanted to speak with her. As she left her cabin, I smiled and looked up from my armchair. She looked at me puzzled but followed Skrog to the Control Center. I joined her as she entered the open hologram.

The scientist sat there and spoke in a wooden tone. "Ms. Omm, I think you may have misunderstood our last conversation. The herbs do exist and are maturing well on the surface of Jupiter. I would welcome you to conduct your study of them and report the results to TESVG. I understand you have a scheduling issue and will not be able to complete the work for a month or, maybe two, but you can be sure that I will cooperate fully with you."

H spat out the words and concluded, adding, "Your captain is a very persuasive man."

He terminated the call, and Flama turned to me: "He'll have to stop selling the herbs when I start the project. After I submit my report, his sponsor will take control of harvesting it, and his nefarious activity will come to a halt. He has a couple of months to cover his tracks but won't be charged with any crimes. It's not a perfect solution, but it's not bad. And I keep my job with TESVG. How did you pull that off, Hut?"

"Call it bribery. If I had used a physical threat, it would have been called extortion."

Kul Lum's Speeder, a Cessna spacecraft that could fly faster than most other ships, came into view on my screens. I marveled at its sleek appearance. It was a beautiful vessel, particularly compared with my tractor. For space travel, an aerodynamic design is unnecessary but the designers at the aircraft company had decided that customers who could afford to buy or rent a Speeder, wanted an attractiveness like those found in science fiction videos. It was a polished dark metallic grey with a nose narrowing to just a few centimeters. It used twin ion thrusters similar to those on my ship but significantly smaller and the craft could achieve a speed that allowed it to cover the distance from Earth to Jupiter in just ten days.

Kul and I would meet face-to-face on his ship or mine. Whichever we chose, we needed a way to move from one ship to the other, and the solution to this was standard on all spacecraft. It comprised a sky bridge that was extended by each ship and connected. At the joining point, both vessels had airlocks that would open to allow safe access between the ships.

Kul's crew activated the Speeder's bridge, Skrog extended ours, and we coupled. In a synchronized action, each vessel automatically opened its airlock.

Kul called over.

"Hut. Let's meet on my craft. It's more comfortable, I'm sure."

Flama picked up on the dynamic. "Having the meeting on his territory puts you at a disadvantage. He's trying to take control."

I nodded. She was clever.

She followed up. "I'll come with you. A second pair of ears might be useful." I thought of Skrog who had four ears himself but I did not comment on that.

"Agreed."

She looked at Skrog. "What about Skrog?"

Normally, I would have taken him with me, but Kul's Speeder was unlikely to be fitted out with seating or other facilities for someone the size of the Martian, so I told him we were leaving him in charge until we returned.

When Flama and I crossed to Kul's ship, it was obvious that no expense had been spared in its construction. The main lounge was three times larger than mine, and its walls were clad with dark mahogany paneling and stainless steel inlays. Expensive artwork was hung on the curved walls, and high-end armchairs and couches were laid out. They were deep, comfortable, and upholstered with the best sustainable leather. It was also clear that the lounge area was equipped with the latest technologies. Real windows, quite unnecessary, lined the walls.

I decided to start the conversation on an upbeat basis. "Very nice ship, Mr. Lum. I see your bosses are prepared to spend a lot on their senior executives." I did not know if Kul was a senior executive, but he preened a little when I spoke these words.

"Hut, I'm a contractor. Cal Rena, the CEO of World Energy, uses me for important projects. I am a sort of fixer. Oh, and please call me Kul."

He extended his hand in greeting and then his eyes went to Flama. "Who is this lovely person? Part of your crew?"

"She is a passenger on a cruise with me."

He smiled at her and then sneered at me. "A cruise? You offered her a pleasure cruise on that rusting tub?"

Flama smiled back at him. "I'm not on a pleasure cruise. I'm a biologist and I'm researching fungi that grow in space tractors and how they evolve."

"Perhaps, my dear, you would like to look for fungi on my ship. I'll bet you won't find as much but it'll be of a higher quality."

She gave him her biggest smile. "That might be nice. Mr. Lum. My name is Flama."

"Please, call me Kul."

I glared at her before realizing that she had seen through the man and was playing him. He did not seem to have noticed and signaled to a steward. His smile continued as he turned to us. "Drinks?"

My dislike for the man had not changed but his offer of a drink seemed too good to turn down. "What do you have?"

A human, not a robotic, steward stepped forward, underscoring my judgment of the high cost of the rented Speeder.

The steward rattled off a list of the best liquors in the System, and I chose a rare, single-malt Scotch whisky. Flama declined, waving him away.

I said to Flama, "Ms. Omm, you wouldn't like a high-end gin?"

She did not hesitate in her refusal.

Kul took his seat in an armchair obviously designated for whoever was in charge of the vessel. It was elevated by an inch or two over the others in the lounge. He waved for us to sit on a couch opposite him.

He started by talking about his various experiences and peppered this with a few questions to show interest in us and to indicate his sincerity. It was standard TESVG Social Demeanor 101 and was wholly transparent. He wanted something. Although I had told him that, as the captain of my tractor, I would make the final decision about the project, Kul focused his attention on Flama.

"Flama, my dear. What is such a beautiful woman like you doing in space? You should be gracing the halls of Earth in Paris, London, New York, or Beijing."

Looking at her, I saw she was not buying his spiel.

As he spoke, I drank about half the Scotch the steward had poured me. It was very good. Very good indeed. I was about to compare it with Galactic in my mind but shut down that idea.

I interrupted him. "This is nice, Kul, but can we get down to business? You have offered a substantial fee but still have not told us what you want us to do."

"It's straightforward. You fly to an asteroid in the Belt, load a quantity of metal there, and ship it to Earth."

"A single trip?"

"Yes. I estimate that it will take nine or so standard pods. You have ten, don't you?"

"That's right."

Kul sat back and then took up a printed document from a side table.

"This contract covers the project, please take a look and then sign it." He called over a robot to witness my signature.

I looked it over for a few minutes and passed it to Flama. Kul showed his surprise at this gesture but I also observed that he was still looking her over, not as an adversary but, I judged, with a more personal interest.

Flama read the document before handing it back to me. Meanwhile, Kul motioned to the steward to refill his glass. He did not offer me more Scotch.

On the third page, I noticed an area of emphasis that was absent from any other shipping contracts I had ever encountered.

I addressed it directly. "You stress that the ownership of the shipped contents is the property of World Energy Corporation and, specifically, that I have no claim to it regardless of any laws or rights I might have."

He looked down at his drink and nodded slightly.

I continued, "That's usually a given in freight contracts. Why spell it out and have a separate signature block for that particular clause?"

Flama's eyes widened, showing her surprise that I had picked up something that she had missed.

Kul started to show a little anger. "Listen, Hut, I'm offering you a lot of money to make this shipment. And we need it fast, so I can even swing a bonus. But I don't want you getting cocky and trying to be smarter than me."

I shrugged. "Kul, the contract's probably fine but let me have a half hour. I'll have to finalize shifting the timescale for the ice delivery to do this for you, as well."

He lost it. "I don't believe this. You agreed to the deal when I was still on Earth. Now nearly two weeks later, and after me traveling for that entire time, you're having second thoughts?"

I had his attention. "Tell me the details of what you want. The contract says I will go to an unspecified asteroid, load about nine containers of refined metal, and transport it to Earth by the fastest route. I need more. Which asteroid? What is the metal? And, also, who owns it? The contract states that it's World Energy, so I assume they do."

He was stunned and no doubt, thought that I would accept the money, sign the document, and do whatever he wanted. He motioned to the steward to refill his glass again. He still did not offer me another. He nodded at Flama, but she declined a drink again.

He said slowly, "The asteroid is Delta23 and the metal is Delt."

"That's a key element of battery technology," I stated, as the memory of my boyhood research project flooded back into my mind.

He blinked. It was obvious that he had not expected me to know about Delta23 and its magical metal.

I gestured to the steward who smiled and poured me another Scotch. It was so good after the years of drinking little other than Galactic.

I looked over at Kul. "Nine pods of Delt would power every battery on Earth and even on the colonies with lots to spare. But the Grid is already in place. So why do you need it? And why the rush?"

Then the news brief I had seen on Canot40 flashed into my mind. I said, "The outage in Germany?"

Kul looked away and I continued, "The batteries in the Grid are failing. Right?"

He was defeated and hung his head. Then, through gritted teeth, he said, "Listen. I am offering you a lot of money to do the run. And I can probably even pay that bonus I mentioned. Sign the contract."

I picked up the document that was in paper form, which was also strange, and put down my empty glass. "Ms. Omm, my second-in-command and I will discuss this and give you an answer in half an hour. In the meantime, you may want to confirm your new offer."

Flama and I crossed the bridge back to my tractor and I briefed Skrog on what was happening. The Martian bubbled. "Sound like lot of World Dollars, Cap. Retire. Get back on gravity land."

Flama was beside herself. "What's going on, Hut? Do you think the Grid is falling apart? And what is this Delt?"

I grinned. This was something that she did not know and I did.

"Darling, surely you know about Delt."

"Would I be asking if I knew?"

I smiled but hesitated before telling her.

She snarled. "Okay, smarty-pants, you know something that I don't. This is important stuff and you need to read me in."

We were sitting in my lounge, but Flama rose and started to pace. The size of the area limited her actions and she let out a grunt, threw up her hands, and retired to her armchair. "Alright. So, it looks like, somehow, the Grid is failing and that is a problem. So how does this Delt come into play."

I told her about my TESVG project, the role of Delt in modern batteries, and the huge amount of refined metal still stacked up on Delta23.

I added, "It looks like they want to replace the current Delt, and Kul's reaction seems to verify that assumption."

She then asked, "All that seems clear but why the special clause? If World Energy mined and refined the metal so many years ago, why are they concerned that we agree that they own it? So odd. Wait a minute." She had thought of something.

As Skrog and I discussed other parts of the contract, Flama called to her wrist computer and, with a series of voice commands, accessed a dozen or so articles and research papers. Then she said. "Got it. Hut, this is what I thought I remembered, and I was right."

One of the wall screens displayed a document. It was a story from a well-known Legal Journal about a case taken to the World Court.

It described a suit dated 2075 brought by the World Environmental Council against World Energy Corporation. The Council insisted that World Energy initiate a cleanup of the mess they left on Delta23, which had been idle for nineteen years.

World Energy did not want to incur the cost and hassle and used the argument that China Mining, not World Energy, owned the asteroid's metals. Since that company no longer existed, World Energy argued that it had no obligation to fund the work.

As has been the case for a century or more, dozens of lawyers, now bots, filed suits calling for some other party to take ownership and be responsible. The World Court bots were frustrated by the myriad of suits and eventually ruled that the asteroid, and anything on it, belonged to no one and, as such, no one was obligated to clean up the site.

The article hinted that World Energy might have put pressure on one of the human Supreme Court judges to drive this decision, but nothing was ever proven.

Flama interpreted the ruling. "This means that the refined supply of Delt on the Delta23 belongs to no one. Anyone can claim it. That's why Kul wants us to sign the clause making World Energy the owner of whatever we find. He doesn't want us to stake a claim."

I leaned forward. "So why doesn't World Energy just make a claim?"

She read more about the case and then said, "The World Court decided in a separate ruling that to claim ownership of metals on non-earth planetary bodies, a person or corporation must physically take procession of it, load it for transport to another planetary body, and provide proof of procession to the court."

Flama's face revealed that she had an idea. More than that, it indicated that she had a sneaky idea. "Hut, darling, if we go to Delta23 and lodge a claim with the World Court, the Delt will become yours. We can ship it to Earth and auction it for trillions."

I looked at her, "Darling, that's immoral."

Skrog bubbled. "Yes. Is immoral. But perhaps."

I snarled at Flama and then at Skrog. "I'm not sure we should do that. We have no right to claim the Delt. It really belongs to World Energy."

Flama laughed, "Grow up, Hut. This is not a game. Legally, you can claim the Delt; if the Court agrees, you own it. You'll be rich and can live a life of luxury. You wouldn't be stuck on this tractor for the rest of your life."

Her words hurt me as she clarified that she found life on my tractor unacceptable over the long term. I knew this already, but her statement stung. I made up my mind. "Okay. Let's go to Delta23. Let's claim the Delt, and let's get rich."

TRANSCRIPT - CCS-00491-29768
 Cessna Speeder
Jupiter Orbit
February 23, 2091/1:12 P.M.
Classification: Originally marked Personal - recoded Business

One side of the conversation only.

Kul Lum: "Steward, get me a holo with NAME REDACTED at World Grid. Classification personal. And fill my vodka. You're slacking."

PAUSE

HOLO-CALL INITIATED

Kul Lum: "We have a problem, sir. Hut Mur has caught on to what we are doing. I'm not sure he'll accept our offer, but I did propose increasing his fee. Is that okay?"

PAUSE

Kul Lum: "Good. But he still might not accept it. He seems smarter than his TESVG grades show and he has a bitch woman with him who is very smart. They may have realized that they can go independently to Delta23, file a claim for the Delt, and sell it to us, or some other bidder, for a huge price."

PAUSE

Kul Lum: Yes. I have researched other freight options and there is one other freighter in the area. But Hut Mur can get to Delta23 before it.

PAUSE

Kul Lum: "One thing I can do though is fly to the asteroid myself and lodge an interim claim for the Delt. My Speeder is a lot faster than Mur's rust bucket. For the final claim, the metal must be loaded to a freighter chartered by the claiming party. However, an interim claim should work and then we can use whoever we want to ship it to Earth."

PAUSE

Kul Lum: "Of course, I know that I have a formal agreement that World Energy will become the owner of the Delt. I shall claim it on behalf of the corporation. You can trust me, sir. But, this extra effort will require more work on my part."

PAUSE

Kul Lum: "That's very generous, sir."

Chapter Twelve

Although, at the time, I did not know what Kul Lum was plotting, I thought that it was likely he already had a Plan B but if not, he was probably working to develop one. Logically, he would be looking for an alternative freighter, so I decided to check out that idea.

I spoke to the system. "Navigation Command." The blue light flashed. I smiled. It was a good start.

"Search for cargo vessels that are close to Delta23 in the Asteroid Belt."

"Found, Hut." Navigation's French accent was always soothing even when relaying a message that could be devastating.

"Are there any ships closer than us?"

"No Hut."

Good.

"Which are the top three closest."

"Other than your tractor, only one is near."

"Distances? No. Days to travel at maximum speed for my ship and the other to reach Delta23. Round answer to whole days"

"Your vessel will take ten days. The nearest other cargo vessel will take seventeen days."

"What about Kul's Speeder?"

"A Speeder will take six days."

"What information do you have on the other freighter?"

"Spacecraft has designation Tractor T175."

Skrog looked up the identifier for the vessel and rocked back and forth. "Not good, Cap. Captain Mak Poh."

"Rats!"

I knew of the freighter and its captain.

Mak Poh was a convicted criminal and had assembled a gang of others like him. They toured the Solar System picking up jobs that embodied elements of illegality. The rumors were that there were about twenty ex-military on board T175. My wrist computer showed me that the ship was a newer vessel and larger than mine but I still wondered where twenty, or so, soldiers would sleep on a tractor built with just six cabins.

There was little crime in space, and settlements and freighters plied their way from planetary body to planetary body without the threat of such. Based on this, the World Council had funded less than one hundred Space Marshals, and most of these were headquartered on Earth. Only a handful were stationed at small administrative offices in each outpost, so I knew that if Mak Poh and his gang became involved, the situation would be messy. We would have no chance of calling for help from the marshals.

I accessed more information on Mak Poh. It was not pretty. He had been discharged from the military force in the States of Central and South America, for murdering civilians in 2057, and for the past 34 years, he and his men had traveled from planet to planet committing a series of criminal acts. Although they operated from a space tractor, somewhat like mine, this was mainly a front for their illegal activities.

While researching this book's transcripts, I found a holo call from Kul Lum's Speeder. Although part of it had been encrypted, I used a decryption app to provide the entire dialog.

TRANSCRIPT - CCS-00491-29770
Cessna Speeder
Jupiter Orbit
February 23, 2091/1:12 P.M.
Classification: Originally marked Personal - recoded Business

Holo-call Monitored.

Kul Lum: "Hi. My name is Kul Lum. I understand you have a tractor available for haulage. Is that true?

Mak Poh: Perhaps.

Kul Lum: Perhaps?

Mak Poh: What do you have in mind?

Kul Lum: I have a project that will interest you."

Mak Poh: I'll decide if it interests me. Tell me what you're looking for.

Kul Lum: I need to keep the contract secret.

Mak Poh: Most of the projects I have executed have been secret. I have no problem with that.

Kul Lum: Good. I was afraid that might not be the case.

Mak Poh: Okay. So, what is this mysterious contract?

Kul Lum: I don't want to discuss it over the holo and I'd prefer to meet face-to-face.

Mak Poh: I can secure our conversation if you wish.

Kul Lum: But that's illegal, isn't it?

Mak Poh: Yes, but it'll make our holo-call secure.

Kul Lum: No. I'll fly and meet you in person.

Mak Poh: I'm not going to wait around for days. It might be a wild goose chase and I am a busy man. Encryption or I pass.

Kul Lum: I wouldn't say I like it but okay. Implement your encryption module.

ENCRYPTION ACTIVATED BY PARTIES TO CONVERSATION

ENCRYPTION DECODED WITH AI-DECODE 731 BY VOICE RECORD CORPORATION, ARGENTINA

Kul Lum: The contract is to load some metal ingots on an asteroid in the Belt and transport them to Earth. An easy job.

Mak Poh: If it's that simple, why the secrecy? What is this metal? Gold?

Kul Lum: No. It's just scrap metal. And what does it matter to you?"

Mak Poh: A lot of secrecy for some scrap metal. I want more details.

Kul Lum: Alright, the cargo is Delt. It's sitting on Delta23 in the Belt and needs to be loaded and transported to Earth. It's of minor value, but my boss wants more of it available. He's an impatient man, which is why we need to get this done expeditiously.

Mak Poh: And who is his impatient man? Or better still, who does he work for?

Kul Lum: My client is World Energy

Mak Poh: Oh. They're huge. So how much are you offering?

Kul Lum: Two million world dollars.

Mak Poh: That puzzles me. Why so much?

Kul Lum: Why should you care? Can you do the job or not?

Mak Poh: Okay. But I want one million paid into escrow now.

Kul Lum: That's fine. I'll fly to Delta23 and secure the load. When can you reach the asteroid?

PAUSE

Mak Poh: Navigation says I can be there in seventeen days.

Kul Lum: That'll work. Anything else?

Mak Poh: This is all very mysterious, and I wouldn't say I like mysteries. You had better not try to screw me.

Kul Lum: I don't like your attitude, but let's focus on the job. I'm delighted to be working with you. I'll send you the contract to sign.

Skrog slid into the Control Center faster than I had ever seen him move. I imagined his twenty toes on each foot pulsating as he came towards me.

"Cap. Kul Lum starting engines. We not agree contract yet so why he start?" He answered his question, "He going Delta23. Claim Delt."

I shook my head. "That won't help him. He needs a way to transport it to Earth…" But the answer became clear. "Damn. I'll bet he contracted with Mak Poh!"

Flama stamped her foot, which is quite difficult in the ship's artificial gravity environment, but she managed somehow. "We have to stop him. If he gets there first and claims the Delt, we'll lose everything. We must do something."

Skrog came up with the solution. "Bridge still attached. Kul cannot leave without releasing his bridge from our bridge. Speeder has new, safety technology. Both ships must disconnect simultaneously. If he try without our disconnect, Speeder locks bridge in place and prevents him engine engage."

Flama waved her arms about and paced up and down. "Don't we face the same issue? We can't break free either if he doesn't release us. It's stalemate."

A short-range holo-call interrupted the conversation. It was Kul. "Hut, please command your bridge connection to simultaneous disconnect. I'm going to fly on ahead and secure the Delta23 site."

I challenged him. "You want to lay claim to the Delt, don't you?"

He hesitated and I knew his answer. Then he followed up. "Of course not. But, if I'm there, I can protect our joint interests."

Skrog caught my attention. He motioned to one of the ship's screens.

"Just give me a minute, Kul." I stepped out of the hologram and read what was on the screen. It was a space map showing in three dimensions the location of Poh's ship relative to Delta23.

Skrog pointed at the image of the craft. "Cap. If Kul does deal with Mak Poh, they go Delta23, and Poh steal Delt from him. Mercenaries bad lot."

Flama had not been in our earlier discussions about Mak Poh and his men, so she looked at the Martian. "Mercenaries? There aren't many mercenaries on Earth and none in space."

Skrog wobbled. "Wrong Flama. Not well known. Skrog come across several times. Bad humans."

I continued to view the map. Other than us, the mercenary vessel was still the only one close to the asteroid. I stepped back into the hologram. "Kul, there is another tractor near Delta23. I suggest you don't consider using them instead of us."

"Hut. You have not been very obliging and have queried the contract despite the huge fee I'm offering. I can use another freighter if I want to, and they seem only too willing to take the job."

I did not hesitate asking, "Is your alternative T175?"

He paused but then shrugged. "Yes. It is. What of it?"

"What do you know about its captain, Mak Poh?"

"I believe that that's his name, but we haven't met."

"Do you know that he's a criminal? A mercenary? And he has a bunch of cut-throats on board?"

Kul's body language showed that he did not know this, but he blustered, "Bullshit, Hut. You can't trick me."

Skog had retrieved an account of a recent battle on Pluto involving the mercenaries. He inputted the video into the hologram, and we watched the action, with Poh's men butchering a small group exploring the remote planet. The footage had been taken from security cameras on the group's Speeder. Mak Poh was identified as the gang leader.

The blood drained out of Kul's face.

I followed up. "Does he know how much the Delt is worth?"

"No. Well, probably not."

I was now in control. "Do you have armaments?"

"God, no. This is a Speeder, not a Defender. I don't even have a hand weapon."

"Have you arranged to meet him there?"

"Yes."

"Even if you lodged a temporary claim, Poh will just load up the Delt and fly off with it."

"He wouldn't do that. Would he?" Kul showed his fear of confronting the mercenary.

"Yes, Kul. He would. And he'll not want any loose ends so he'll, no doubt, kill you and your crew."

Kul was now very scared. "I'll contact my boss and have him send a Defender with a squadron of World Guard or Space Marshals so we can arrest him when he arrives."

Skrog was not in the hologram and wobbled. He spoke to me without Kul being able to hear him. "Defender not get to Delta23 in time. Too far from Earth. Mak Poh get there first."

I nodded and waited for Kul to respond. Kul must have had his crew make their calculations. He echoed the same conclusion about the Space Marshals' arrival and showed his concern about dealing with the mercenaries. He said, with a shaking voice, "Perhaps I'll just return to Earth. Disconnect your space bridge, and I'll blast off." I knew he was lying.

I stood in the hologram and instructed Skrog, "Skrog, implement simultaneous disconnect for our bridge." Skrog knew that I did not want him to act on this request. The words were for Kul's benefit.

Kul indicated that he was happy with my order and spoke with more confidence than previously. "Thanks, Hut. I'll call in the request for a Defender and then head back to Earth. I'd still like you to go to Delta23 and collect the Delt."

He did not speak of the additional bonus we had discussed, and I knew he was not to be trusted.

Skrog left the Center and I watched him on one of the screens as he slid across the space bridge to the point where the two craft were coupled. Decoupling is a simple matter. The two bridge mechanisms are activated simultaneously from the control center of each vessel, and for a new Speeder, this was the only approach incorporated.

My older ship, however, had a manual override, which allowed Skrog to close our airlock and withdraw our bridge without closing the Speeder's airlock. In doing so, he triggered an error message on the Speeder. This automatically closed the Speeder's airlock and threw a lock on the bridge mechanism. This "safety feature" would prevent the Speeder's crew from retracting their bridge. Safety protocols prevented engaging the Speeder's engines while the bridge was extended. Kul could not leave his current position in space until it was unlocked.

Kul's engineers would be able to override the locked bridge, but it could take them days and require manual work in space. If they were closer to Earth, the normal procedure would be to call a repair ship, but out here, a spacewalk was the only option. Regardless, we would beat him to Delta23.

I watched as Skrog implemented the operation and heard, over the holo-call, the alarms sounding in Kul's Speeder. Looking surprised, he spoke with someone on board and then turned back his face red with anger.

"You bastard, Mur. I'll get you for this, you two-bit asshole."

His voice recorder kicked in. "Kul Lum, you are fined $200."

I sat in my control seat. "Navigation Command." The blue light did not flash, as, once again, the system failed to pick up my command.

Flama was in the Control Center with me and echoed my wake-up command.

She said, "Navigation Command." The unit flashed blue and spoke, "Bonjour Flama. How may I help?"

I narrowly avoided an expletive fine and gave my order. "Navigation Command. Develop course to Delta23."

Her soft, feminine, voice responded. "Okay, Hut. Done. ETA March 6 at 10:15 a.m. Travel time nine days, four hours, and twenty-seven minutes.

I turned to Flama. "How come Navigation picks up your voice but not mine?

She smiled. "Perhaps you mumble."

I snarled and said, "Operations Command. Accept course and drive."

As always, there was no great revving of engines as heard in many of the fiction videos, but a slight shudder as the ion thrusters reached power and then accelerated, driving us towards Delta23, the medium-sized asteroid I had read about thirteen years before. I had never visited it but now it had become a focal point in my life and I wondered how my adventure would play out.

Would Delta23 be the place where I ended up?

Chapter Thirteen

TRANSCRIPT - CCS-00491-29771
Cessna Speeder
Jupiter Orbit
And
World Power Grid Headquarters
Nuuk, Greenland
February 28, 2091/1:12 P.M.
Classification: Originally marked Personal – recoded Business

Holo-call

Kul Lum: I have terrible news, sir.

Grid Executive: What now? Where are you? Delta23?

Kul Lum: No, sir. I'm still in Jupiter orbit. My ship suffered a failure and my crew have just now solved the problem.

Grid Executive: Okay. So, what about the Delt? Did you get Mur to agree to the contract?

Kul Lum: Well, no. He realized what it implied. I think he's flying to Delta23 to lodge a claim.

Grid Executive: What? Do you know what that means? Over the years I've trusted you to solve problems and now, it seems, you have created a new one.

Kul Lum: I am truly sorry about that, sir.

Grid Executive: Anyway, fly to the asteroid now and negotiate the transfer of ownership. Downplay the value of the Delt. Use all the sneaky skills that you've honed over the years. Threaten lawsuits. You know the sort of thing.

Kul Lum: I'm not sure I want to go to Delta23 just now.

Grid Executive: What? Why not?

Kul Lum: The alternative carrier we found is a mercenary who is traveling with a group of criminals. They are already flying towards the asteroid.

Grid Executive: And they know about the Delt? And its value?

Kul Lum: I believe so. Not exactly but in a call, I had with them, they certainly knew a lot. Searching Worldnet is not difficult.

Grid Executive: What do you think is going to happen?

Kul Lum: I don't know, but Hut Mur and his people will reach the Delt first, lay a claim, and load it to their cargo pods. The mercenary, Mak Poh will probably arrive there about the time loading is complete. The two of them will fight and Mur will lose.

Grid Executive: Go there. Sort it out.

Kul Lum: It's too dangerous. I'm not risking my life for a contract.

Grid Executive: So, this Mak Poh claims the Delt, and we pay a ransom for it? Your work is done. Your contract is terminated. Don't expect to work for World Energy ever again, and don't expect to be paid for this job either.

The trip from Jupiter to Delta23 would take nine days and Flama and I settled into a cozier relationship. She still exhibited some criticism and dissatisfaction, but we enjoyed countless hours in my cabin and hers.

However, on the third day, in the middle of the night, she prodded me, and shook me awake. Although I had come to terms with this foible, I still found it annoying to be woken from a heavy sleep.

"Hi Flama. What do you want to talk about?" My head was drowsy, and I wanted to quickly end the conversation, which I knew was coming, and return to my slumber.

"Hut, our sex is so good. You implied that you had not had many relationships and yet your skills are formidable. I don't understand."

I had not told her about the sex worker on Saturn6.

My brain was still half asleep and I mumbled, "I guess it's just instinct. Now, go back to sleep."

"I can't believe that it's just instinct. There must be another explanation."

I was starting to dose off and did not reply immediately.

"Hut, are you listening?"

I struggled to think of what to tell her and decided that the truth would appear sordid. "I watched a lot of videos. They'll teach you everything these days. It certainly wasn't Tes."

"I don't believe you. It was an affair with someone else. Wasn't it?"

I was drifting off again but desperately tried to answer her question and return to my slumber. "Instinct and videos. Now, go to sleep."

"Not credible, Hut Mur."

"I'm going to sleep now. I suggest you do the same. Let's talk in the morning."

"I can't sleep when this is on my mind."

"You're so serious and fixated. And you never laugh at yourself."

"Why would I want to do that?"

"It's a skill that humans have. It's not a big thing if you feel secure. We all make mistakes and accepting them and laughing them off, is a strength."

"I don't get it."

I dozed off and she hit me. "Wake up. You can't just criticize me and then nod off."

I do not have a quick temper, but being woken up about something trivial did not sit well with me. "Flama, we'll discuss this in the morning. Go to sleep."

"Asshole."

"Flama Omm, $100."

The next morning, she returned to the subject but I maintained that my skills were a mix of instinct and videos. She made it clear she did not believe me but let the matter drop.

She stood up from the armchair in which she had been siting and started an attempt to pace around the lounge area. She motioned me to move my feet twice and then commented, "I'm bored."

I tried to smile at her and said, "Want to watch a video?"

"A sex video?"

"No. Something entertaining."

She seemed to brighten. "What do you have in mind? I don't want some action thriller."

"How about something rather old? Before you could change the plot and mood of the show. Before holographic videos."

"Might be interesting."

"One that I like is *Casablanca*. It's in black and white and was made in 1942. It's a love story set in World War 2."

"Never heard of it."

"Want to try it?"

"Sure."

An hour and a half later as the movie was finishing, Flama turned to me. "That was so beautiful. I think I'm going to cry." She leaned over and kissed me tenderly. "Have you ever been in love, Hut?"

I looked at her and decided that a flippant answer would be inappropriate. "No. There are not many girls in space, and I have never had the opportunity to fall in love. Frankly, it scares me. How about you?"

She tucked her legs under her. "I've tried but it never worked out. The closest was a wealthy guy. Real estate. He wanted to grow his business and own the world. He was self-centered and just wanted a token girlfriend. I ended up hating him."

She motioned to the end credits on the *Casablanca* video. "Do you know of any more videos like that?"

I turned on all forward cameras and looked out at the barren asteroid, Delta23. We had arrived at the shapeless terrain pockmarked with millennia-old craters where meteorites had hit the atmosphere-free surface and I easily picked out the huge quarries that had been dug symmetrically across the planetoid. My research told me that there were five underground refineries where the Delt had been separated from the mix of ore and other material that had been mined, but it was not easy to identify their entrances.

I shook my head. The asteroid's surface was a wasteland, littered with old machinery worn and damaged by the hazards of space and the twenty-four years it had remained silent and unused. It was a mess and I found myself supporting the World Environmental Council's unanswered demand that it be cleaned up.

Before preparing to fly down to the surface, I checked with the Navigation system.

I was careful to speak clearly, and loudly. "Navigation Command." The blue light flashed.

We had left our Jupiter orbit eleven days previously and I asked Navigation the same question that I had repeated several times on our journey. "Has Kul's Speeder been able to retract its space bridge yet?"

"Affirmative, Hut."

"When?"

"Two days ago."

There was no way that Kul could have beaten us to our destination.

I instructed Navigation Command, "Tell me the location of Kul's ship."

"Speeder on course for Earth, Hut."

I did not know Kul's motivation for abandoning the project, but I assumed he did not want to face Mak Poh and his cutthroats and decided to return to Earth.

I turned to another, more pressing question. "What is the trajectory of space tractor T175?"

The system answered immediately. "En route for Delta23."

I groaned. I had expected this, but the confirmation made me feel nauseous.

"ETA?"

"March 14 afternoon Eastern Time."

That was in eight days. It was going to be tight. We had to find the Delt, load it, and depart the asteroid before Poh reached us. The alternative was a fight and they were armed. We were not.

Flama heard the interchange and recognized the problem. She shook her head. "Hut. You've told me these people are pirates and killers. What chance do we have? Shouldn't we leave the Delt and run?"

I turned and looked at her. "The metal is worth a fortune. I'm not prepared to give up." I didn't need to add that Poh would become rich and we would remain poor, living on a secondhand space tractor.

I spoke clearly. "Navigation Command" and the blue light flashed. "Do we have sunlight in the areas we have targeted?"

"Yes. Sunlight started on that part of the asteroid two hours forty minutes ago and will continue for another four hours and thirteen minutes before the area is shrouded in darkness."

I said to Skrog, "Let's get to work. We don't have a lot of time."

Skog and I pulled Grade A space suits from storage lockers and helped each other climb into them. We connected the helmets and the oxygen tanks and were ready to go.

Skrog looked at his attached computer. "Tanks good for six hours. Is enough and hope we don't need second trip."

Flama looked us over. "What about me?"

With my helmet in place, I used my inbuilt radio but knew that my voice coming out of the ship's speakers would be hollow and sometimes distorted. "Grade A suits are custom and we don't have one for you. You'll have to wait here while we check out the site. You can talk with us through the mike on the console. Just say 'Communications Command, talk'."

She uttered a grunt of exasperation but accepted the reality of the situation.

Skrog and I took the shore boat and motored to the surface. Having researched the site on Worldnet, I could not find any maps or other details of the facility other than that the Delt, after being refined, was smelted and poured into ingots of two cubic meters. We had accessed pictures of towers of the refined metal, and these had to be somewhere on the asteroid, probably in a below-ground warehouse.

We touched down in an area with barely visible markings, which designated it a landing area. After twenty-four years and being frequently struck by other, smaller asteroids and meteorites, the site we found was pitted but clear of major debris, so the landing was simple and safe.

Delta23 is only one hundred kilometers across and has little gravity, so Skrog and I used an old-fashioned approach to prevent us from floating off into space. We jackhammered a series of bolts into the surface and attached each of us to them with long titanium cords. This made moving about cumbersome, time-consuming, and, frankly, annoying.

At the edge of the landing site, we located a small building with a door that probably led down to one of the underground facilities. It was locked.

"Clever. When they left the asteroid for the last time, they locked up after themselves." But for my immovable space helmet, I would have shaken my head.

Skrog selected a tool from a collection he had brought with him and prized open the door. It was dark inside and our headlamps automatically turned on revealing a staircase leading down into the ground. Using a handrail to anchor us, we descended and found a group of walls surrounding some structure. There was an airlock that was not operational, and I assumed that, back in 2055, the interior had been pressurized. An artificial atmosphere and gravity would have enabled a more tolerable environment. On the door was stenciled, in fading paint, Refinery 3.

Skrog wobbled. "Not here. We need warehouse for Delt, not refinery. Must be another place." It was just as well since gaining access would have needed greater effort than we had available from our hand tools.

We located two other underground refineries and saw that a track led from each to another part of the asteroid.

"Path lead warehouse, Cap. Delt stored there."

We followed the path to a doorway, cracked it open, and looked inside. A steep ramp led into a vast warehouse stacked high with towers of Delt ingots. The metal was a dull grey and did not look interesting or valuable, but we knew differently.

As we flashed our lights over the hoard, my mind went to videos I had watched in which adventurers discovered buried treasure.

I voiced my thoughts over our radio system. "Bingo."

Skrog bubbled inside his helmet. "Bingo indeed, Cap."

Flama, on board the tractor, was listening to our conversation. "I gather you've found it."

I answered her. "Yes. And it's obvious that they stored it ready to be shipped to Earth before the refinery management learned that the first load was sufficient and a second wasn't needed."

We gazed up at the towers of the metal ingots on pallets for loading. I conducted a rough count and concluded there were about 10,000 of the two cubic meter slabs.

Even though his face was partly hidden by the mirrored face mask of his space suit, I saw that Skrog was bubbling. "Easy loading, Cap. All set up. Nice."

The ingots were secured to the pallets with titanium wire, but we needed to break the towers down for optimal storage in my cargo pods. We used some of the tools we had brought with us to release the tethering on the palettes and then returned to my ship. The weight of the metal ensured that the ingots did not move despite the low gravity of the asteroid.

"So?" Flama was beside herself. She was annoyed that we had not been able to take her with us and frustrated that she only had voice communications with Skrog and me.

As Skrog helped me remove my helmet, I answered her question. "Piece of cake." It was an old-fashioned expression, and no one today knows its origin but it implies that something is easy. I described the warehouse and the towers of Delt to Flama and showed her some videos we had shot.

She regarded the images with relish. "Great. We'll need these when we lodge our claim." As I had expected, she queried me. "Okay, Hut. You found the Delt but how do you load it to the pods? If you and Skrog have to carry each ingot separately, we'll be here for twenty years."

I laughed. "The magic of drone robots, darling."

I saw her beautiful eyes open wide. "You have drones?"

"Yes, my love. In the aft storage bay next to the thrusters." I continued, "But first we have to move the pods down to the surface so they can be loaded."

Skrog and I worked with Operations Command and less than an hour later we had positioned all ten pods on the asteroid on a site that had probably been used for a similar operation some twenty-four years previously.

After this, that same day, we accessed our main onboard computer and input the parameters that our AI loading software app needed to control a squadron of unmanned vessels. Each drone was large, about nine meters by nine meters, and had eight arms. We ran a test, having one fly down to the surface, enter the warehouse, bundle up twenty or so ingots, strap them into a block, and load them into a pod.

A few things went wrong, and we adjusted the program accordingly. After the fifth attempt, the process worked smoothly, and we unleashed the other drone robots.

Flama let out a chuckle and hugged me. "Darling, that is amazing. I think you are a rocket scientist."

If I had not been wearing my pressure suit at the time, I would have puffed out my chest.

The loading would take about a week so, while this was happening, we started making an ownership claim for the metal with the World Court.

The claim procedure had been developed by bureaucrats years previously and implemented by low-level AI programming bots. The questionnaire and forms we needed to complete, had a degree of personalization but since the registration system was designed for a broad set of claims, it was not easy to use and some data, that was classed mandatory, was not relevant and not available. Flama volunteered to work with the system and did so exhibiting a patience that I did not have, punctuated by fits of screaming desperation, and anger.

We supplied video images of the ingots on Delta23, the drones at work, and the filling of my cargo pods. We added references to the court orders regarding assets from the asteroid and a shipping manifesto, which completed the documentation that the program required. Then, as I half expected, a request came in for several of the same documents, and we sent them again.

The process took two days, and we finished receiving a documented filing certificate duly approved by the World Court. We now owned the Delt and the loading of the cargo pods was nearly complete. We only needed nine pods so we left the final one empty.

Something had been bothering me, so I voiced my question: " Now that we have the metal and officially own it, how do we sell it to World Energy?"

Flama laughed. "We contact them and negotiate a price."

The original contract amount offered by Kul Lum was for transporting their metal to Earth, but now that we legally owned it, the price we could demand would be much higher. I made my announcement. "I'll negotiate. I've done this for a bunch of shipping contracts and I always get a good, but fair, price."

Flama looked at me in disbelief. "Did you say 'fair'? Don't you get it? This is not a transportation fee we're asking for. Our claim has been ratified by the World Court, and we now own the Delt. It is ours to sell."

I shrugged. I knew all this.

Before I could add to the discussion, she continued. "Although the media has not discovered the problem yet, the market has detected something about World Energy and their stock price is down about 9%. The World Council is probably going crazy because if all the batteries in the Grid fail, the world will enter an economic meltdown like it's never seen before, even during the War in 2047. Millions of companies will fail and billions of the population will die. Mobile communicators will stop working. The world needs the Delt for survival and we have the only supply of it. Its value is a lot more than just a transportation fee."

Wow! I realized that she was right, and I started to contemplate the sort of sum we might be able to negotiate. It was probably tens of millions of dollars.

She accessed archived records and whistled. "Back in 2060, China Mining established a value of half a trillion dollars for it. With our historic inflation rate that would be over one trillion in today's dollars."

I was amazed. One trillion dollars?

She continued. "And at that time, the metal was not proven to work. It is now, and the world will come to an end without it. We'll start the bidding at six trillion and certainly not accept less than three."

Skrog bubbled and added, "World Energy Corporation has revenue of two hundred trillion so three trillion small amount for them."

Flama looked at me and stated directly, "I'll handle the negotiations. Not you. Okay?"

I looked back and nodded.

"Say it, Hut."

"Okay. You'll handle the negotiation, Flama."

While the drones were finishing loading the Delt, Flama started the discussions with World Energy. Initially, the corporation's contact was a manager from their Purchasing group but Flama insisted that she would only deal with the CEO himself. Cal Rena.

For the first call with this man, she wore her designer pressure suit. She enhanced it with a red, neck scarf. I stood back from the hologram but was ready to step in if she wanted me to.

She opened the call. "Mr. Rena, I am pleased and honored to meet you. World Energy Corporation is a fine company, as is your subsidiary, World Power Grid. We are delighted to be doing business with you."

She was standing in the hologram and the CEO of World Energy was sitting in an expensive chair in his New York office. Flama continued. "My name is Flama Omm, and I represent Hut Mur who has claimed the supplies of Delt from the asteroid and has them in his possession."

"Claimed? What do you mean claimed?"

"Yes, claimed. We filed all the documents including photo images and video and our claim was accepted by the World Court. The confirmation number is D23-4791373. Hut Mur, now, legally owns the Delt."

I watched the man's image closely and tried to decide if he had been genuinely surprised by our successful claim or whether he already knew about it and was starting his negotiation game. I am still unsure, but I suspect it is the latter.

He continued, "Ms. Omm. This is unacceptable. World Energy owns the Delt and your claim is without merit. You're attempting to steal the metal from us."

He paused and gave her a broad, patronizing smile. "However, if you complete the transport of the product to Earth, I shall pay you your usual transportation fee with a bonus of 50%."

"Ha. Nice try, but no chance. As I said, the claim has already been ratified. Although, I expect you know that."

The CEO's face turned red with anger, but he managed to control his feelings and adopted a fixed smile.

"Ms. Omm, we shall contest that ratification in court and my lawyers will make mincemeat of those law bots that you employ. And when the court finds that you have no rights to the metal, I'll have you arrested on a felony charge of attempted theft or trying to extort my company."

Flama stood her ground. "If you choose to fight the claim, even if you win, the Delt will be held by the court for months, perhaps a year while all the appeals are heard and decided. Can you afford to wait that long?"

The CEO's face twisted into a snarl, but this shifted to one of a reluctant acceptance of Flama's point. She continued not deviating from the business at hand. "We have nearly finished loading and will shortly commence transportation of the metal to Earth. You will have what you need within a few weeks. If we can agree on a price, you'll be able to start the swap out of your depleted batteries after that time."

The CEO exhibited, what I took to be genuine surprise. "What do you know about the battery depletion? Did Kul tell you?" He was almost beside himself.

"No, Mr. Rena, we deduced that ourselves."

She paused for a moment and added, "We have also reached out to several other companies, on a confidential basis, and they have expressed interest in purchasing the metal should you and I reach an impasse on price." I looked at her. Was she lying? Of course, she was.

The CEO looked down and mumbled something inaudible. Flam asked, "Mr. Rena, I couldn't hear that."

He looked up and spat the words into the holo-call. "How much do you want?"

Flama gave him a number and he blanched. "You must be joking."

I was proud of her and saw the World Energy CEO twitching.

The discussions took several rounds and lasted two days. Flama was relentless, pushing Cal Rena time and time again, but a price was finally agreed upon.

The amount she extracted from him was incredible. She wrapped up the negotiation. "My bot has drawn up a contract and sent it to you for electronic signature. Do that and initiate a transfer of 50% to an escrow account, and we shall start the trip to Earth."

Then she added, "We'll classify the Delt as scrap metal. That way the transaction tax withheld will be only 5%."

Rena snorted and after a few fake pleasantries, Flama terminated the call.

"Well, Hut. We did it. You are very close to being the richest man on Earth."

"Congratulations, Cap."

I understood the classification ploy. "Thank goodness, we don't still have income tax."

From the early eighties, Earth had stopped taxing personal income and corporate profits and instead adopted a system based on what people or companies expended - a transaction or sales tax. This was much easier to implement and regulate since all transactions were now cashless. When people buy goods or services, the price includes tax. Basics, food staples, simple clothes, and rent for housing, healthcare, and energy carried a low rate with higher rates on what was classified as luxury items.

As I thought about my new wealth, a broad grin spread over my face.

Chapter Fourteen

I was feeling better than ever before. I had a beautiful and smart girlfriend. I would soon have nearly five trillion dollars in personal wealth. The last Delt ingots had been loaded, and we had brought the cargo pods back into space. What could go wrong?

The Navigation system shattered my happiness.

The feminine French accent spoke calmly, "Hut, scanning reveals tractor designated T175 in the range 200,000 kilometers with trajectory directly towards us."

"Shit."

"$100 fine,"

"What is it, Hut?" Flama had also heard the message. Then we received a holo-call.

The hologram showed me a tall man with muscles bulging from his military-style pressure suit. There were three others visible in the image and they looked just what I believed them to be. Thugs.

Their leader hailed me. "Hello. My directory shows that you are Hut Mur, the captain of that ship. Right?"

"Yes. And I'm pleased to meet you. You're Mak Poh aren't you?" I said this cordially despite my feelings of concern.

"Let's cut the crap, Mur. I know about the Delt and that World Energy is prepared to pay a lot for it. I don't know why they want it, but I don't care either."

"Really? Delt? Is that a designer clothing line?"

"Enough. You know what it is, and you know it's worth millions of World Dollars."

"It is? If it is valuable and if I do have it, would you be interested in buying it from me?"

"Fat chance." I saw him consulting his control panel. "My sensors tell me that you have already loaded it into your cargo pods, That's great. We don't travel with containers, and I was worried that we would need to have someone bring them up while we safeguarded our possession of the metal."

"Your possession? I've news for you."

"What's that?"

I knew what I was about to say was unlikely to change the situation but I said it anyway. "We have already lodged a claim and it's been approved and ratified by the World Court. We now, legally, own the Delt."

"Why should I care about your stupid claim? My intention ought to be clear. I'm going to take your precious metal from you. You probably regard that as stealing but stealing is what we do."

He laughed, and his cronies in the holograph with him echoed his merriment. He stopped laughing and adopted a serious expression. "Now, Hut Mur, unhook your trailers, and we'll hook them up and take them to Earth. We'll leave you here in peace."

I said, "Nice try, but what makes you think I'd agree to that?"

He hesitated for a moment before saying, "We can do this the easy way or the hard way. In the easy way, you and your crew won't get hurt. But my guys are always up for a fight so the hard way would work for us as well. By the way, you seem to have heard of me. Perhaps my reputation is well known in the space haulage business."

"Well Mak, as I just told you, we have made an ownership claim with the World Court, and it has been ratified. We own the Delt."

"Oh, Hut, my friend. Ownership is in procession. If I take the metal from you, it's mine. The World Court stuff doesn't matter."

"You know this is all being recorded don't you."

"Of course it is. But, frankly, I don't care. The authorities are after me for more serious crimes and an extra one, or several, won't make any difference."

He let out a laugh. "And when I have the Delt, no one will give a damn. I'm starting to realize, that this scrap metal is pretty valuable. World Energy, or whoever will agree to whatever price and terms I dictate."

I knew he was right but he had implied that the metal was worth millions not trillions, so, clearly, he did not know the Delt's full value.

Flama had also picked up on Poh's undervaluation of the Delt and whispered to me. "Try agreeing to what it's worth and splitting it 50:50. We don't cause him any trouble and he gets half for doing nothing."

I looked at her in disbelief. I guess she had little real-world experience and thought that an agreement between two men would be honored. Perhaps if they were honorable men, it would be, but maybe not even then.

I whispered back, "He'll kill us either way."

Her face turned white, and my mind raced to think of a solution.

"So, Mak, tell me more about the hard way."

He laughed and then convulsed in an extended fit of laughter. "Hut, you idiot. We'll outrun you, pull alongside, and ram your craft. We'll puncture your hull, and your ship will deflate and you'll all die. Then, I'll take the pods and proceed to Earth. Take the easy route. Unhook your pods and fly away. Poor, but alive."

Flama screamed. "He's going to kill us."

I whispered back to her. "That's what I just told you."

Skrog wobbled as my mind raced. Tractors are built strong to allow them to sustain minor collisions when they move trailers about and navigate in confined areas. A tractor ramming a Speeder would destroy its flimsy hull in seconds but that is not necessarily the case with another tractor. I thought of some extra technologies I had installed that would help us.

"Okay, Mak. I'm calling your bluff but may the record show that you instigated this conflict. If you suffer from it, it'll be on your own head."

"Hut Mur, you are an idiot as I said before. Alright, let the fight begin." He terminated the call.

Flama buried her head in her hands. "Oh God, Hut. We're going to die."

"Not yet. What do you know about warfare, Flama?" She gave me a withering stare.

In my TESVG studies, one range of subjects I liked a lot related to Warfare, and the course that I liked most was battle strategy. In the course, some battles were ancient and some modern. However, many of them boiled down to similar tactics, and I seized on one single success factor from many of those conflicts. Force your enemy to fight on a battlefield of your choosing.

I spoke. "Navigation Control." Nothing.

Skrog spoke to the system and the Navigation flashed its blue light as it responded to his voice. "Bonjour, Skrog. What can I do for you?"

Before he could answer, I issued an order. "Lay in a course for Delta23. I want us very close to the surface. I don't care where."

"Course laid, Hut."

I attempted another voice command. "Operations Command." The blue light flashed. Phew.

"Accept Navigation's course. Prepare to accelerate to that position but wait for my order to engage drive."

The British accent from Operations said, "Confirmed, Hut."

I visualized Mak's next moves and assumed that he would see my ship's movement and suspect we were attempting to outrun him and escape. He would probably try to ram us as soon as possible so he could salvage my cargo pods and start his journey to Earth.

Skrog sat in his control seat and looked over the array of sensor data before him. "Ready go, Cap."

I instructed the system to engage the engines and was delighted that my first voice input was accepted. The ion thrusters started and my ship lumbered forward trailing the ten trailers behind it. We gathered speed and, just five minutes later, we were close to our destination about 10,000 meters above the asteroid's surface.

Skrog was tracking Mak's tractor. "Mercenaries coming behind us. They will avoid trailers. Attack our tractor only."

Of the ten pods that I towed, only nine were needed for the Delt, and the final one in the chain was empty.

I explained my plan to Skrog and Flama. She, immediately, started to find flaws in it. I snapped. "Flama, I am the captain of this vessel, and I don't have time to discuss alternative approaches. I have made my decision and we are going to live or die by it. Understood?"

"Die by it?"

I knew she was furious, but I did not need her lack of experience in space, and life at this juncture.

She grimaced but nodded her head, "Yes, sir, Captain," and sank into a seat behind us in the Control Center.

"Skrog. Their position?"

"Coming up fast. Will align with pods in three minutes."

"Advise when his ship is two hundred meters behind pod number 10."

Two minutes passed and then Skrog told me what I wanted to know. "Mak Poh in position now."

I decided that I had no margin for error which might occur if the voice command system failed me, so I switched to optical keyboard input.

"Operation Command. Execute five successive 20-degree turns from left to right," I keyed.

As my craft executed the maneuver, the pods behind swung back and forth, with the last one swinging much more than those nearer my tractor. As I observed, on my monitoring screen, the tenth pod's path brought it close to Mak's tractor as he was overtaking us. I nodded to Skrog and, as the pod swung even closer to Poh's ship, he issued the command, "Release coupling pod ten."

The unleashed container accelerated through space and struck the back of Mak's vessel as it passed. It appeared to be just a glancing blow.

"Check the damage to Poh's vessel, Skrog."

"Roger, Cap."

The Martian ran a few diagnostics and said, "Okay hit. Fusion exhaust crushed. Not lethal. Will not take out of game, but certainly damaged."

A call came in. I opened the channel.

In the hologram, Mak stood there and was furious. He pointed to Hut's image and shouted, "You asshole." The recording system broke in, "Mak Poh. You cannot use expletives in holo-calls. Fine assessed is $100."

This did nothing to calm the mercenary and he released a stream of curses which resulted in his credit accounts on Earth being depleted by over one thousand dollars.

"Sorry, Mak. But you did say you wanted my trailers."

I terminated the call, and we watched the screens. Mak was obviously worried about the pod's damage to his tractor and performed a series of maneuvers to assess its reduced capability.

Skrog gave me his assessment. "Poh's ship still work well but not full speed, Cap. If we ditch pods, we might be able outrun. If we keep them, we cannot."

I had hoped for a better result, but I still had a few tricks up my sleeve.

"Prepare to detach the remaining pods, Skrog."

Flama said quietly, "Hut, you're giving up the Delt?" I was about to answer her when she continued. "But, I guess, if he gets it, he'll have no reason to kill us." She seemed happier now. "And if he couples up the containers, he won't have the maneuverability to ram us. Right? We'll live through this."

I shook my head. I expected Poh to ram our ship before he hooked up the pods that would soon be floating unfettered in space. However, I had something entirely different in mind, and I gave Skrog a grin.

I keyed some commands into the Operations system.

Skrog looked at his screen, read the instructions, and bubbled. "I understand plan, Cap. I ready airbag."

Flama raised her eyebrows. "Airbag?"

I laughed. Skrog had understood the plan perfectly.

I spoke clearly, "Operations Command. Detach remaining pods." I was hoping the system would take my command. The blue light flashed, and the pods were set free.

A few minutes later, we received another holo-call from the mercenary ship. "Thanks for the cargo pods, Hut. Unfortunately, I don't want to have you and your crew accusing me of grand theft, so before I hook them up, I'm afraid you all must die." The hologram flicked off.

Although I had expected this move, it caught Flama by surprise. "He's going to kill us anyway?"

I nodded. "That's his plan. There was never any possibility that he wouldn't. Now, we need to decide if we want to try to outrun him. Or do we fight him and reclaim the pods?"

"Fight him? Are you mad, Hut?"

On our screens, we saw Mak's ship alter its course directly in line with the right side of our vessel. Skrog wobbled. "He ram us, Cap. Estimate two minutes 15 seconds."

Poh's tractor accelerated towards us and Navigation Command showed that he had targeted the front of our vessel.

Flama panicked. "We're going to die."

I tried to calm her. "Buckle up, sweet thing."

"Don't call me sweet thing."

Skrog and I had already attached our usual seat harnesses and now added the additional leg, neck, and head braces. Flama emulated what we had done, and I glanced over to make sure that she was secure.

"Are seat restraints really going to help us, Hut?"

"It won't hurt."

"God, there are still times when I hate you, Hut Mur."

We watched the screens as the attacking craft bore down on us.

Mak came through in another call. He was sitting secured in his harness. "Hi Hut Mur. Your little attempt to damage my ship did nothing. It's working just great. Nothing personal but goodbye." He appeared exhilarated and his grin filled the hologram.

I spoke quietly to my system. "Holo-call Command. Retain image and audio from Poh but mute ours."

"Activated."

I became silent and waited. Thirty seconds passed, but it seemed like minutes as Mak's tractor bore down on us.

Flama screamed at me. "Do something. He's going to kill us."

"It's okay, Flama. Everything is under control." I hoped it was.

A minute later, when Mak's ship was just three hundred meters away, I shouted "Operations Command, deploy the right airbag." Nothing happened. Bloody audio.

Skrog used his short, stubby fingers to enter a few keystrokes into the system. When Mak's craft's forward bumper was within one hundred meters of us, our screens showed a huge Teflon fabric ball blasting out of my vessel's right side and inflating.

I crossed my fingers.

"What the hell is that?" Flama whimpered.

"It's an airbag. It's a feature I added as a safety device, but I've never needed it before. It's like a fender and designed for emergency collisions like striking an on-planet mooring pylon."

Skrog called out. "Operations Command. Engage left bow thrusters, forward and aft. Full power."

My tractor started to slide sideways toward Mak's vessel.

"The thrusters will push against Poh's ship and help counteract the force when he tries to ram us."

As she was behind me and I was concentrating on the control displays, I could only imagine her hands shifting to her face as she cried out. "Oh, God!"

I watched the screens and nine seconds later, Mak's spaceship hit the airbag.

Despite the power of our bow thrusters, we were jolted severely and without the seat restraints, we would have suffered significant injuries.

However, my vessel was unharmed since the airbag performed as I had hoped. Mak's tractor's forward path was halted and his ship, literally, bounced away.

The hologram showed Mak still in his restraint but others in his gang, who had not expected the impact, and not belted in, were thrown from side to side and fell to the floor. Their cries rang out as their craft tumbled away. Although we had been jarred from the collision, my ship was stable and undamaged. Mak's, however, flipped over several times. I could see his actions and hear his voice commands as he tried to regain control of his spaceship, but the damage we had already caused to the rear fusion exhaust system prevented the vessel from righting itself. Had we been in open space, Poh might have avoided his fate but, with Delta23 just 10,000 meters below, his options were limited and the damage to his craft's exhausts cut his maneuverability further.

A minute later, it flew down towards the asteroid, and Mak Poh uttered his last screams as his tractor crashed into the wasteland. Another relic was added to the pockmarked surface of Delta23.

"Oh my God." Flama watched several of our screens show the ship crumple, and it was clear that Poh and his gang would not be troubling us or anyone else again.

The tactic had gone better than I had hoped and I grinned. "Piece of cake."

Skrog rolled all six eyes, and Flama gave me a look that told me she was trying to decide whether I knew what I was doing and had executed a clever ploy or had lucked out.

I continued to grin at her and she seemed to make up her mind. "Hut, darling. That was masterful! What a great maneuver. I'm impressed. I so…" She started to shiver which I took to be a reaction to the shock we had just experienced. I waited for her to complete her thoughts but she turned away and smiled at Skrog before leaving the Control Center.

Skrog leaned forward and whispered to me, "Very luck was with you, Cap."

I whispered back, "I know."

I decided to find out why Flama had left us. "Skrog, deflate, and re-stow the airbag and hook up the cargo pods. Let's go to Earth and make a shit-load of money." The voice monitoring system rebuked me with a fine of $100.

$100? Who cares? I thought.

I left the Center and walked back to the lounge. Flama stood there. Her eyes, those beautiful blue eyes, were shining but I saw that she was still shivering. Shock?

She came over and placed her hand on my arm. "Hut. I was so scared. But it was so exciting. I started out doubting you but you were so…in control."

I smiled at her.

She looked at me. "I feel hot."

I was confused. "You're hot? But you're shivering."

She kissed me long and hard. "Idiot. Hot. I need you now. Help me out of my pressure suit?"

An hour later, we were flying towards Earth, and Flama and I sat in the lounge toasting my victory over the mercenaries and Flama's win in negotiating the deal with World Energy. Not to mention some amazing sex.

Chapter Fifteen

Delta23 and Earth rotate in their orbits, and the distance between them varies dramatically. However, I was lucky. For our passage to Earth, these heavenly bodies were largely aligned, and the distance to Earth was only 415 million kilometers. My ship was not as fast as a Speeder, so it would take more than a week, and this time would allow me to reflect on my relationship with Flama.

The day after we started our trip, I sat in the Control Center, and Skrog slid in, taking his seat next to me. He looked over, and I said, "We have about eight days to reach Earth, and I have an idea for a project that we might use to fill in the time."

"Sound interesting, Cap. What you want me do?"

I explained my thoughts and he bubbled. "Sound good idea. I like."

We spent the next half hour discussing the details before I rose and made my way back to the lounge.

That morning, Flama had left my cabin and seemed to be in a contemplative mood.

She had a serious look on her face, and I wondered what was going on in her mind. I reached out and placed my hand on her arm. She shrank back from my touch.

I asked her, "What's wrong? We have just about everything. Money. Safety from Mak Poh and his men. On the way to Earth."

She looked away. "I'm going to my cabin." She left and although she closed her door behind her, I noticed that she had not engaged the lock.

I sat down in my usual chair and attempted to work out what was happening. I thought about knocking on her door, entering, and taking her in my arms. But I was afraid of her reaction. She's probably just exhausted from the excitement. Tired, I thought.

Instead of going to her, I made the wrong decision and decided to leave her alone until she calmed down.

The clock on the wall told me that it was 4:00 PM but I muttered the words from an early century song I knew, *it's five o'clock somewhere*, and poured a Galactic. It won't be long before I shall be drinking high-end whiskey as I had on Kul's Speeder.

Skrog joined me and I poured a glass for him as well.

He sensed that something was wrong. "You not happy, Cap. Where Flama?"

"In her cabin."

Skrog bubbled. "She dressing?"

"No." I added, "We didn't."

His eyes darted back and forth. "What wrong?"

"I don't know. She's in a bad mood, I guess. She'll be fine."

When the clock indicated that it was 6:30 PM, a half hour after we usually met for our evening meal, I said, "I wonder if she's skipping dinner."

Skrog slid towards her door, "I ask her."

A few minutes later, Flama joined us, and I noticed that, unlike most evenings, she had not changed her clothes or showered. Both were out of place. "Are you alright?"

"Fine. Just fine."

Skrog leaned forward. "I cook tonight. Special treat."

I tried a joke. "I know. It's grilled chicken."

She did not laugh.

Skrog continued, "Tandoori Shrimp."

I asked Flama, "Gin, or do you want to go straight to wine?"

"Just water."

I was starting to feel a wave of anger rising.

"Listen, darling. If Skrog is going to the trouble to make a special meal, you could at least seem appreciative."

She glared at me, smiled briefly at Skrog, and left for her cabin. This time I heard the lock engage.

The next morning, Flama appeared and looked worse than if she had been drinking the night before.

"You look terrible, Flama. Are you sick?"

She gave me a snarl, which I remembered from our early days. "I'm sick of being on this …" She spat out the word "…tractor."

I lost it. "Flama Omm, give me a break. I'm sick of putting up with your gripes and snide comments."

"But you like having sex with me."

"True but your attitude is making me wonder if it's worth the effort."

"You don't need to worry about that. I'm not sleeping with you again."

I grunted. What is wrong with the woman?

I decided to talk to Skrog about the situation so I rose and walked to the Control Center where he was reviewing the operating logs.

I entered and took my seat next to him. He wobbled, and I knew he was about to tell me something serious—hopefully not about another potential catastrophe.

"Cap, what relationship you and Flama?"

I was surprised. Skrog had rarely asked me any personal questions.

"What do you mean?"

"Are you love her or just sex?"

Shit, I thought, but avoided a fine by not saying the word aloud.

His question had caught me at a time when I was contemplating the same issue.

I replied, "I think it's love."

"Do you know how she feel, Cap?"

"No. And I'm worried. I think she thought she had feelings about me but I think she has changed her mind and is going to dump me."

Skrog looked away and wobbled. "She come Skrog and talk me about it."

"Really? What did she say?"

"She confused."

I was taken aback. "I don't understand. She has gone back to the bitchiness that she had when she first came on board."

Skrog turned his body and fixed me with all six eyes. "Flama worried to be what she call 'gold-digger'. She has wanted mate who is rich and with the sale of Delt, you are now candidate. She not happy with you when you tractor captain but now you rich, she worried you think she will take advantage."

I shook my head. "I don't get it. She didn't want me when I was poor, and now that I'm rich, she still doesn't want me. Maybe it's my intelligence. Maybe I'm not smart enough for her."

"She not mention that. She has strong feelings for you but scared of commitment and possible breakup. She not want to hurt you."

"I see."

"Remember she talk about previous relationships. She play men and dump them. She afraid that she do to you."

I was starting to become annoyed. "Has she considered that I might drop her? Before she has a chance to walk away?"

"Yes. She mention that too."

"You have lived nearly one hundred years longer than me. What's your advice?"

"I think you two good together. I think close. I think you have future together."

"There are times when I can't stop thinking about a life with her and there are others when I feel like throttling her."

"Relationships have good times and bad times. Need work."

"What about you Skrog? Have you had many relationships?"

"In space it difficult. I had few but only one was right. It ended bad. She daughter of current High President and was childhood sweetheart. High President wanted her to be with higher ranking Martian, not number two on tractor. Communicates still. Not in relationship."

Skrog had not shared this side of his life and my heart went out to him.

That evening before dinner, I stood and addressed the two of them. "I've been thinking." Flama scowled and Skrog leaned forward interested in what I was about to say. "I have given a lot of thought to the proceeds that I will have from the sale of the Delt." Flama looked away. "The amount is well over whatever I could spend in a lifetime even with the transaction tax on luxury goods, so I've decided to split the funds equally between each of us. We each get a third."

Flama's mouth gaped open. "Really? You want to share? Each of us equally?'

I smiled at her.

Skrog bubbled. "Very generous. Simple split. Good. Thanks to you, Cap."

Flama adopted a serious look. "It's your ship and you're transporting the metal to Earth. I thought you might share it with Skrog but with me?"

I grinned. "You've earned your share with the World Energy negotiation, Flama."

We would be, equally, the richest three beings on Earth, provided we could deliver the Delt to World Energy.

As Skrog poured drinks to celebrate, I played through in my mind how Flama would react to this. With my newfound riches, she could have partnered with me and taken advantage of it. Skrog said she had not wanted me to think of her as a gold-digger and maybe, this was at the heart of her recent behavior. Now, she would have her own wealth and if she continued our relationship, it would be for its own sake. She now had a choice. She could stay with me, or she could take the money and leave. I closed my eyes and did not want to think about that possibility.

Over the next few days, Flama was polite but aloof as she joined Skrog and me for meals but spent most of her time in her cabin. I decided that my best path was to ignore her. This was the wrong approach! I became used to the idea that when we reached Earth, we would each go our own way and she would find some other poor sap to torture. Regardless, I was about to become ridiculously wealthy, Mak Poh was no longer a threat, and the trip to Earth was proceeding without incident. What could go wrong?

After breakfast on the fourth day, Skrog slid in and motioned to me.

"Need talk, Cap."

"Okay. How can I help?"

"Go Control Center, Cap."

He breathed deeply a few times, an expression that was the opposite of bubbling, and I knew he had some bad news, so I stood up and followed him.

When we were alone, he wobbled. Never a good sign. "Well, Cap. Skrog in dilemma."

I gave him a serious look. "Go on."

"Receive message from uncle on Mars. He difficult. Knows we have Delt."

I was shocked. "How could he know that?"

"Has contact in World Power Grid. Scientist. Uncle know we transport Delt to Earth and huge value." Skrog looked down with all six eyes. "Uncle has other idea."

"Your expression tells me that I'm not going to like this."

Skrog wobbled before continuing, "Martians feel oppressed by humans. Uncle wants use Delt to blackmail World Council for better rights. Move population from Mars to Earth, as was promised years ago."

I was stunned. "But he doesn't have any Delt."

"He want steal from you."

Just then, Flama entered the Control Center and caught the last part of the conversation. "What are you saying, Skrog?"

Skrog took a few deep breaths. "I not know what to do." He tried to hang his head as he had observed humans doing but since his neck was just an inch or two in length, and the same size as his head, he was unsuccessful. Instead, all of his eyes looked down at the floor.

I groaned. "So how are your people going to steal the Delt from us?"

Using all six eyes, Skrog looked at Flama and me, four on me, and the other two looking at her. "Wait until cargo close to Earth. Board your ship. Take charge. Armed troops." He added, "They want Skrog operate sky bridge."

I looked back at him in disbelief. "Armed? How can they be armed? No one is permitted to have weapons anymore."

Skrog rocked back and forth. "You forget Martian agreement with Earth. Before 2048 global gun control, Earth agreed we have right to defend ourselves."

"This doesn't sound much like defense."

Flama rose and started pacing about the Center. I found this annoying since the area was small and she seemed to constantly trip over my feet. She let out a huff. "We have to find a way of stopping them."

"What do you have in mind?" My stress level had returned, and her vague comments were irritating.

She said, "I don't know. Fight them."

"Great plan. Perhaps I'll offer them a duel." I couldn't help being sarcastic.

Skrog continued to rock back and forth. "I don't know how solve problem. I do know I not desert you and Flama, Cap. My loyalty with you both. Must find way stop them."

If I had been able to, I would have hugged him, but my arms would never reach about his girth and I would injure my back stooping to attempt the embrace.

Flama stopped pacing. "I have an idea."

I was cynical. "Okay. What is it?"

After she explained it, we agreed that it might work, and since no one had a better option, we accepted Flama's plan.

Over the next hour, Skrog made a series of calls to the Martian government including one to their High

President. He used his own language, and I could not understand any of the dialogue. And I certainly cannot write it down in this account.

After the last call was terminated, Skrog spoke to us in English. "Deal agree, Cap."

Flama stood in the hologram and Skrog and I sat just out of its range.

She started her conversation with the World Energy CEO. "Greetings, Mr. Rena. I wanted to give you an update."

He grunted. "Do you have the Delt?"

"Yes. It's loaded and we're on the way to Earth.

"Good news, Omm. What's your ETA?"

She told him and then added, "Oh, sir. There's a little change that we need you to agree."

His body language showed he was both suspicious and annoyed. "What?"

"I understand that World Energy has a solid relationship with the World Council and to ensure the Delt reaches Earth expeditiously I want to request something from them."

He was now angry, but Flama continued. "The Martian relocation has been languishing for years and the agreement for them to relocate to Earth must be tabled and agreed in the next few days. Before we hand over the Delt."

He appeared puzzled. "I thought you and Mur were just adventurers but now you seem to have a political agenda."

"Think what you want. That's the deal."

"But why? What do the Martians have to do with this?"

"They have an armed vessel heading towards us and they plan to steal the Delt and use it to blackmail the Council. They'll trade the metal for the land on Earth they were promised in 2049."

"Steal the Delt? Rubbish. The Council will call up a Defender or two and stop them."

"If they do that, they'll start a full-scale war with the Martians. Do they want that?"

"They'll see these demands as extortion."

"Probably. But the Martians comprise a threat and ratifying the land deal will secure your metal and make them very appreciative. Think positive. One hundred thousand new customers for the Grid."

The CEO paused for nearly a minute. "I'll talk to the President and see what he can do. But, young lady, this is the last little game you're playing with us. We had an agreement, and I am not going to renegotiate every few days."

"This was not our doing, sir. We have identified a problem and are offering a solution."

Chapter Sixteen

TRANSCRIPT - WWC-97431-62175
World Energy Corporation HQ
New York
and
World President's Office
Singapore
March 17, 2091/9:02 A.M.
Classification: Originally marked Personal - recoded Business

Holo-call

Cal Rena: Jom, it's great to talk again.

World President: Maybe. Is your company's battery issue solved? It hasn't hit the press yet, but if you can't sort this out before it does, I may not be able to help you.

Cal Rena: It's under control. The tractor driver has confirmed ownership of the metal and is transporting it to Earth. The problem is he wants a lot of money.

World President: And you don't want to pay him.

Cal Rena: Correct. If we do, it'll affect my bonus, not to mention the little arrangement that you and I have.

World President: Be careful what you say.

Cal Rena: I know.

World President: What do you have in mind?

Cal Rena: Once we take procession, I plan to file a lawsuit accusing them of extortion, treason, or something.

World President: What you do regarding the tractor driver is of no interest to me. Just keep me out of anything that might be considered corruption.

Cal Rena: Agreed. A suit will save World Energy a lot of World Dollars. But there is just one other matter, Jom.

World President: I somehow knew there would be.

Cal Rena: It's the Martians.

TRANSCRIPT - WPO-99431-62935
World President's Office
Singapore
March 17, 2091/4:12 P.M.
Classification: Originally marked Personal - recoded Government

World President: Damn it. This is a mess. We finally have a solution to the battery issue and now, some two-bit space cowboy and the Martians are holding World Energy to ransom. And, Cal Rena has dragged us into it.

World Vice President: I agree. It's a problem but there's not much we can do about it. If this Hut Mur hands over the Delt to the Martians, they'll hold the Grid and the rest of Earth to ransom for years. They'll just let us have enough of the metal over time to avoid bringing Earth to a standstill. Whatever we do, the media will find out about it and probably even find out about our personal links with World Energy. That'll be another problem. They'll say our actions have only been to enrich them and ourselves."

World President: Be careful what you're saying. I've designated this conversation 'personal' but the damn system might re-categorize it.

World Vice President: As president, you can issue an order to make it inaccessible.

World President: Yes. And I'll do that as soon as we're finished.

World Vice President: I understand that Rena came up with another option. He'll accuse Mur of extortion. We'll send a Defender with Space Marshals to arrest him and take possession of the Delt. We'll try to do that before the Martians get to it. Even if they have already stolen it, our little green friends won't be a match for a fully armed Defender. The short green people are not going to start a war over this.

World President: If we send a warship, it'll be all over the media. They'll question our right to seize the metal, and the story will be splashed over Worldnet.

World Vice President: We could call it a secret and international emergency. We'll use Section 456.23 for the authorization and class it a felony indictment for extortion prompted by a complaint by World Energy.

World President: I don't like it. Too many people are going to know.

World Vice President: The only alternative is to accept the Martian request. We've always discussed a stretch of land in Mongolia, and they accepted that way back in 2049. We can grant them immediate occupation if they agree to stand down.

World President: That sounds like a simpler approach, and I should get some great ratings from the Left.

World Vice President: Rena's not going to be happy. World Energy is still going to have to pay for the Delt

World President: World Energy can afford it.

World Vice President: Shall I reach out to the Martians?

World President: Yes. PAUSE. On second thoughts, I'll handle the call. Set it up. And I'll make sure that I destroy this recording."

The president did not know that a new version of the voice recording software had recently been implemented. The software searched for phrases like "destroy" or "alter recordings," and the World President's "destroy this recording" comment triggered the system to immediately save the recording to a secure location to protect it from harm.

TRANSCRIPT - WCC-99610-62998
World President's Office
Singapore
and
Martian High President's Office
Mars colony
March 18, 2091/10:30 A.M.
Classification: Originally marked Personal - recoded Government

Holo-call

World President: Mr. High President, it's good to meet again. How is life on Mars?"

High President: Good meet again, Mr. President. Underground city on Mars miserable place to live. We Martians not happy here. I believe we have important subject discuss.

World President: I have never visited your colony but I have traveled to Earth's colony there and I agree with you. Mars is not a pleasant planet on which to live.

High President: So, is that reason for call?

World President: I'm sure you already know what I'm calling about. It's about your people's relocation to Earth.

High President: Continue.

World President: My council and the professionals in government have dropped the ball for many years regarding the agreement from 2049 between Earth and your people.

High President: What "drop the ball"?

World President: I'm sorry. That's an Earth term for "failed to do what is needed". An agreement was made between your predecessors and mine to provide land on our planet for your people in exchange for access to your technologies.

High President: Understand. Continue.

World President: Over the past forty years, you and your people have delivered on your promises. You gave us many superior technologies including propulsion additives and the ion thruster engine which are fundamental to our current space travel. Your people also shared philosophies which we have incorporated into our society.

High President: Seem good deal for your people.

World President: As I said, our side of the agreement was to provide territory on Earth for your people to relocate to and live in harmony with humans. Regrettably, we have not fulfilled that part of the arrangement owing to internal and foolish political attitudes.

High President: This history. Bad. But past. What future?

World President: Today I want to rectify that by formalizing the transfer of 500,000 square kilometers in Mongolia to your ownership. This will be ratified as the Martian Relocation resolution.

High President: Mongolia not best place on your world.

World President: I agree. But that was what was agreed upon in 2049 and was acceptable then. Our climate change has made it more arid, but subterranean water is now accessible, and the land has become fertile and cooler than many other places on Earth.

High President: Yes. Done research. Agree.

World President: There's another matter. I'm told that some of your people are planning to attack and board an Earth spaceship. That must not happen, or this deal is off.

High President: Understand. You need Delt for battery. You do this for man, Rena. He has bought Delt. Yes?

World President: Does the reason matter? Let's concentrate on the outcome.

High President: I stop attack.

World President: Excellent.

High President: How soon is relocation?

World President: One month. All the paperwork has been in place for years.

Shortly after this communication, a member of the High President's staff called Skrog and they spoke for several minutes.

He turned to Flama and me and bubbled. "Deal done. Uncle stopped and Martians move to Earth in next few weeks. High President call me hero."

Skrog settled back in his armchair and proceeded to consume a half dozen whiskeys. I had never been so happy for him as his normal modesty gave way to an expression that reflected his pride in what he had achieved.

"Skrog is happiest being in Solar System. Hero of Mars. Never dreamt possible."

Having finished the bottle of Galactic, he reached into the liquor locker and produced another bottle. He let out his customary belch.

"Flama, Hut. Must join in drinking my achievement."

His exuberance was infectious and both Flama and I raised our glasses in a toast to the four-foot Martian.

Flama was smiling for the first time in days and I found myself looking at her and grinning. She seemed to catch herself and her face started to return to a scowl. But then, she gave her head a toss and the smile returned. It was as if what I thought we had lost we had recovered.

Skrog's six eyes took in the scene and he caught our attention. "Hut, Flama. Both silly people. Both in love. Accept."

That night, we made love and it was different, even better than before. Afterward, I drifted off into sleep but an hour or two later, Flama reached over and prodded me.

"Darling, Hut. I'm so confused."

I was soundly asleep, but her words broke through my slumber, and I knew I had to wake and converse with her.

"Yes?" was all I could manage.

"Yes? You don't care if I'm confused?"

My mind was still hazy. "Go back to sleep. Let's talk tomorrow morning." I heard her snarl and realized that there was no escaping a serious conversation, probably about something trivial.

She leaned close to me. "I have a confession to make."

This comment penetrated and I sat up fully awake.

"Confession?"

"Yes." She paused before asking, "Do you believe in love at first sight?"

I knew this was not a theoretical question and she had my attention. "Maybe." I decided a guarded response was best.

"Well, Hut. I fell in love with you when we first met, back on Canot40."

I was astonished. "So why have you been such a bitch all this time?"

"I don't know. I was fighting it. I have never been in love like this before, and you didn't match what I had looked for in my dream man. I needed to get to Jupiter and you were the only path there. But I knew that being alone with you would be difficult and I felt vulnerable. I knew that if you showed an interest I would probably overreact and our relationship would fall apart just like all of my previous ones. But this time, it would not be me who was calling the shots but you. I decided to alienate you so an affair would not even start."

"But you came on to me."

"Yes. A lapse."

"A rather enjoyable lapse, as I remember."

"I remember too. And the time after the shower incident was even better. But…"

"But what?"

"I'm so screwed up."

"If it helps, I think I fell in love with you when we first met, as well."

"An electric tingle?"

"Yes. Then you felt it as well."

"Yes."

She snuggled up to me and we spent the rest of the night in each other's arms.

The project Skrog and I had started on our trip from Delta23 had not been easy but Skrog had some leverage as an "endangered species" and gained the cooperation of a variety of sources on Earth for our mission.

As we were about to moor off the Moon refueling station, a week after leaving the Belt, we had the answer and I called Flama from her cabin where she had gone to shower and change for our evening meal.

"What do you want?" She was not wearing her pressure suit again and I was about to rebuke her but just shrugged.

"I have a surprise for you, Flama."

"Let me guess. We're having grilled chicken for dinner."

Her expression did not tell me whether this was a joke or an admonishment. I carried on. "Skrog and I have been executing a project. I'm sure it'll interest you."

"I wondered why you two were spending so much time in the Control Center. This ship runs itself and the path to Earth is straightforward." She looked at each of us. "So, what did you discover that I'll find interesting?" Her face revealed that she probably thought our work was some weird science project.

I signaled for Skrog to begin and he bubbled. "When you tell us about your dad, you didn't know whether he guilty of crimes they charged him."

"Yes. That's right. But what's that got to do with your research." Then it appeared to become clear to her. "You researched my father's case?"

I looked gravely at her. "Yes."

"And you have found something?"

"Yes."

The expression on her face showed that she was worried about what we had discovered. Had we found that her dad was guilty or innocent?

I had discussed this probable reaction with Skrog, and we had decided to keep a neutral face at the beginning of the conversation.

After a short pause, she asked, "And? Please tell me. Even if he was guilty, it'll allow me closure." Her voice was hoarse as she choked up with emotion.

Skrog and I held our serious expressions, but he broke it first with a bubble. I broke into a grin. "He was innocent, Flama. Your mom was right. It was his boss, Sus Pagu, who sold the profiles and software to the porn video people, not your dad."

She sat down. "How do you know? How can you be sure?" She paused and added, "Why didn't he tell me he was innocent? Tell mom? Tell my brother?"

Skrog wobbled. "He trapped. Evidence pointed him. Pagu set up. Your dad framed. Porn firm threaten kill all your family if he talk. He hide truth. Save you."

I picked up the story. "Your mom didn't know either but when she suicided, he decided to tell the truth. At first, no one wanted to listen to him and he knew that if he told you about the situation, you would fight like crazy to free him. The Vietnamese would find out and probably murder you. So, he quietly took his own life, without even thinking about the negative aspects of leaving you alone."

Flama started to cry but then raised her head and asked, "How do you know all this? How are you so sure?"

I answered her. "A friend of Skrog, a Martian, works in the WBI."

She interrupted. "The WBI?"

"World Bureau of Investigations - WBI." I continued, "Skrog's friend accessed personal recorder records between Pagu and the Vietnamese company. These came to light after your dad had been convicted. The transcripts showed the conversations were guarded, but it was clear that Pagu had sold them the profiles, not your dad."

"What did they do about it? Anything?"

I said quietly, "The WBI later indicted Pagu but he died mysteriously before his trial. They quietly closed the file. Bottom line, your dad was innocent."

Flama had stopped crying and looked at the pair of us. "You did this for me?"

"Who else?"

I expected her to rush to Skrog and attempt a hug but she turned to me and, walking over, kissed me long and hard. "You know space tractor captain, I'm so in love with you."

That night, Flama and I lay in bed together and she smiled. It was a beautiful smile but then it darkened.

I lost my own smile. "What's up, darling?"

She sat up. "Hut, I love you so much, but I'm scared."

"Scared?" I knew what her fear was.

"Yes. Scared. My relationships have always ended badly. And I have never really been in love before. Will something happen that causes us to break up? Will you get sick of me? Sick of my whining? Or will I lose interest and walk away? Oh, God, I'm so confused."

"You're over-analyzing the situation. You know I love you too and I'm prepared to take the risk. You may be a whiner, but you can learn to stop that annoying habit. I'm sure TESVG has a course for that."

"Asshole."

"Flama Omm $100."

I took her in my arms. "Listen. I have never really had a relationship before. I'm scared of these same things as well. I've spent a lot of time thinking about it and I recognize that things might not go smoothly. Over the years, I have needed to make decisions on the ship which could have been wrong and would have resulted in our deaths. I believe I have good instincts which go beyond smarts and logic. We will work as a couple. You have the academic brains and I have the street smarts. The practical stuff. We're a team. So put your hypothetical concerns aside and let me lead. Trust me."

This was one of the longest speeches I had ever delivered and Flama hesitated before replying. "Okay, Hut. Let's trust your gut feelings. Anyway, I'm getting used to grilled chicken for dinner."

The next day, I entered the Control Center and two of Skrog's eyes swiveled toward me.

Turning to him, I said, "Skrog, may I have a few minutes alone up here?"

"Yes, Cap." He rose and slid out the door closing it after him. His expression would have been difficult for most people to read but Skrog and I were close and I was sure that he indicated that he was puzzled by my request.

I took my seat and stared at the controls.

"Navigation Command," I said the words slowly and loudly. The blue light flashed. It was working.

"Tell me Navigation Command, why are you having problems when I try to activate you?"

Her French accent was normally endearing but now it grated on me. "I was not aware of any problems, Hut. Perhaps you mumble."

"I have frequently spoken the words Navigation Command, and your light has not flashed. You didn't become active." I paused and then added, "I know your system is older than some on the ship, but you seem attuned to Skrog's voice and Flama's. It's just mine that you don't respond to."

Navigation responded immediately. "Hut. If I do not hear you clearly, I cannot become active and have no idea that you want to issue your commands."

I stared at the interface. "It's a problem. Recently, there have been a few times when I needed you urgently, but you did not respond. How can we remedy that?"

"I suppose that you could speak more clearly."

I had started getting annoyed by the system's malfunction, but now I was losing my temper with it.

"That's not good enough. I shall say the wake-up command five times now and the next time I use it, you had better activate. Do I make myself clear?"

"You do, Hut. Say the commands and I shall listen closely and adapt to the idiosyncrasies of your voice."

Was Navigation being sarcastic?

"Navigation Command. Navigation Command. Navigation Command, Navigation Command, Navigation Command."

After the fifth command, Navigation flashed her blue light. "I have recalibrated my system and believe that I have it right now."

"Good."

Standing to leave the Center, I stopped when the system spoke to me again. "I'm sorry about the mix-up, Hut. It won't happen again."

TRANSCRIPT - WPG-29731-41622
World Power Grid (WPG) Research Division
Nuuk, Greenland
March 22, 2091/3:10 P.M.
Classification: Originally marked Personal - recoded Business

Scientist 1: I've been testing another approach, sir, and I have found something that's very interesting and exciting.

Scientist 2: Not now. I'm very busy. The new Delt will be here within a week, and we have to be ready to start the battery swap internationally. A spokesperson from Mr. Rena's office has told the media that we'll be maintaining the Grid. She made it clear this was not a big deal.

Scientist 1: But, sir, everyone believes the batteries don't need maintenance. They haven't needed it for the past twenty-four years, and the press will wonder why we need to do it now. And there's already a rumor. Rena's people are going to need to be very skillful in handling this.

Scientist 2: That's their problem, not ours. But, tell me more about this rumor you've heard.

Scientist 1: One of the networks picked up on it. That there's a shipment of some special metal from space arriving imminently.

Scientist 2: And how did that leak?

Scientist 1: Probably the World Council.

Scientist 2: That organization leaks like an old-fashioned sieve. Well, our PR people will have to handle it. You and I need to get the replacements done and everything back to normal.

Scientist 1: Well, that's what I wanted to talk to you about. There may be another way.

Scientist 2: Another way? Another way to do what?

Scientist 1: There might be another solution that doesn't require new Delt.

Scientist 2: What?

Scientist 1: My team continued testing the depleted metal and experimenting with it. We found that passing a high voltage current through the metal for about twenty minutes reactivates the battery. I've tried it with a hundred or so batteries and it worked every time. Maybe we don't need the fresh Delt after all."

TRANSCRIPT - WEQ-10147-38297
World Energy Corporation HQ
New York
and
World Power Grid (WPG) Headquarters
Nuuk, Greenland

March 23, 2091/1:12 P.M.
Classification: Originally marked Personal - recoded Business

Holo-call

Cal Rena: That's fantastic news, NAME REDACTED. But are you sure? Can we reactivate the batteries?

Grid Executive: Yes, sir. We don't need the Delt.

Cal Rena: Okay. Cancel the next payment to Mur and return the first one from escrow.

Grid Executive: We have a contract with him and we'll have problems retrieving the first payment. He'll surely sue us.

Cal Rena: Let him. We can afford better lawyer bots than he can.

Grid Executive: If we state that he used extortion to gain that first escrow payment, we can have it retroceded and the authorities will send Space Marshals to arrest him. When we needed the new Delt, this wasn't an option as the metal would be held by the courts but since we don't need it anymore, that doesn't matter. Shall I have a warrant issued?

Cal Rena: Yes. Do it.

Chapter Seventeen

We refueled our thruster additives at the Moon station and traveled the short distance to an Earth orbit. Tractors are constructed in space and are not equipped with any capabilities to operate in Earth's atmosphere, so to offload cargo, the tractor moors in orbit, and the pods are transferred to tenders that fly up from the planet. These take them on their trip to wherever they are needed. I took up my position and waited.

Flama smiled at me and lifted a fork of food to her mouth. "I do like the grilled chicken."

I smiled back at her, and my heart was full of what, I guess, is love. I watched her every move. I was enchanted with the way she held her fork to eat, the way she sipped her wine, and the way she sat.

She took another bite of her dinner. "When we get to Earth I'm going to take you out shopping. We'll have more money than we can ever spend and you'll look so good in some of the new designer fashions. Get you into some brighter colors as well. I'll pay."

I groaned.

My wrist computer buzzed, and I saw that I was about to receive a holo-call. The Caller ID showed that it was from a personal assistant in Cal Rena's office, which surprised me. Until then, it had always been the CEO himself who called.

Nevertheless, I walked to the Control Center and answered the call in a cheery voice. "Hello, this is Hut. I guess you want a progress report."

The personal assistant appeared in the hologram and seemed to snigger. "Sure, Mr. Mur. Why not."

I wouldn't say I liked his attitude. He was almost flippant. We were about to deliver refined ore that would save Earth. The man should not have been so glib.

I told him cheerfully, "We can offload the Delt to your space-to-surface tenders anytime. I am in position at the coordinates you sent for the handover." I added, "Since we have reached Earth zone, the first half of the payment is due and I want to make sure you transfer that from the escrow to my personal account. You do have the details of that account, don't you?" My mouth began to salivate, and I grinned at Flama and Skrog who had accompanied me to Control and were standing outside the hologram. My mind raced. Within an hour, I would become one of the richest men on the planet and within a week, as soon as the Delt was accepted by World Energy, I would receive the second payment and my wealth would double.

The assistant gave me a small laugh and I knew something was wrong. He spoke. "I'm afraid there has been a change of plan. We have found that we do not require the metal after all, so I've been instructed to cancel the order. No hard feelings, I hope."

I was almost speechless. "What do you mean? Cal Rena, himself, confirmed that the Delt in batteries around the world is depleted and you need a fresh supply. Or the Grid will crash and …" As I said this, my mind raced. Why don't they need it? Or was this a new negotiating ploy?

The PA answered, "You see, Mr. Mur, we have discovered a simple process for refreshing the current Delt, which means we do not need a new supply or pay you the ridiculous ransom you demanded."

After a short pause, he continued. "Sorry about your efforts to get it here." I could tell he was enjoying himself and then he added, "Oh, by the way, the Court released the escrow account and the first half of your expected fee has been returned to World Energy. We have filed charges of extortion against you and your crew and Space Marshals are on their way to take you into custody. You may want to attempt to make a run for it. Perhaps you can outrun the Marshals." He laughed. "There's no need to thank me for the 'heads up'." He terminated the call.

We took in what we had just heard and Flama used a string of expletives I had not heard her use before. She was fined a record $1,000. Skrog breathed in and out deeply and I sat down without uttering a word. We lapsed into silence which Flama finally broke.

"Think he's bluffing?"

I looked about the lounge. "I don't know, you can read this stuff better than I can. What do you think?"

She breathed out. "I don't think it's a bluff."

Skrog attempted to lower his head as he often did and failed again. "Look bad, Cap. If they refresh Delt then much cheaper than replace. Also, less publicity."

"And the Space Marshals?"

"Not surprise if happen."

Flama threw her hands up. "Have you heard of the penal colony on Saturn? It's not very nice."

I returned to my control seat. "We have a valid contract so we'll sue them." I added, "But they'll tie us up in court for years."

Flama snorted. "Those bastards in World Energy…" The voice recorder interrupted and notified Flama of her additional fine.

She continued. "The agreement we have with them is recorded and binding and if we deliver the Delt, they're obliged to pay us. Oh, it will cost billions in legal fees on both sides and take forever. And they would have this as a potential liability on their balance sheet all that time." She poured herself a glass of water, sipped it, and screwed up her face at the taste. "But, by having us arrested for extortion, they'll probably avoid all that." She gave a short laugh. "I'll bet Mr. Rena is also feeling embarrassed about what we made him agree to pay for the metal. He wants some personal revenge."

I shook my head. "What do we do?"

Skrog wobbled. "Marshals use Defenders. We not outrun that class spaceship. Even if ditch cargo pods, they catch us in three days. Fleeing not feasible."

I added, "And if we scuttle the pods, they'll charge us with Grand Space Littering. That's another five years."

Skrog wobbled more than I had ever seen, and I was worried he would overdo it, lose his balance, and fall. I reached out to him. "Are you okay?"

"Yes. Fine. But upset."

Flam and I both assumed he was distressed after personally losing over one trillion dollars.

He seemed to sense this and then let out what I took to be a snarl. "Deal Earth and our people not happen now. Your president will renege. Martians stay on Mars. Not go Earth."

"But the resolution was passed and is now law."

"Earthlings good at breaking law."

My mind was working overtime. I spelled out scenarios of possible approaches we could take, but none held much chance of success. Then something occurred to me, and I looked at Flama. She looked back, and I knew we had the same thought. Although I did not know at the time, it is not uncommon for people in a close relationship to mirror each other's thoughts and, often, complete each other's sentences.

I spoke first. "I have an idea and it involves our friends, the Martians."

Flama smiled. "I know where you're going." We both looked at Skrog and explained what we had in mind.

Over the next hour, we developed the approach more and checked out its logistic feasibility.

Flama asked, "Can it work?"

I shook my head. "It's going to be tough. But the first move is to get the Martians on side."

Skrog wobbled. "Yes. Many things can go wrong. But I call High President."

Flama sighed. "Okay. Let's do it."

I reached out to Navigation. "Navigation Command. Lay in a course to Mars."

"Done, Hut."

"Operations Command. Engage engines maximum speed."

The slight tremor confirmed that we were moving forward.

Flama called over to me. "A lot will depend on when the Space Marshals' vessel leaves Earth. Can we find out their flight plan?"

Skrog bubbled. "Friend in WBI will tell me."

He made a holo-call to the Martian who had helped with information about Flama's father and then initiated a call with his High President.

An hour later, Skrog reported progress. "Marshals not depart Earth for three days. High President, approve your plan."

"Skrog, we are traveling at maximum speed but, even with the Defender's delayed departure, they will still catch us. Check with Navigation when that will be."

Navigation Command listened to Skrog's orders and loaded the flight data into her system. The conclusion was not great. "Look tight, Cap."

※

Seven days later at a position 300 million kilometers from Earth, Navigation alerted me.

"Attention, Hut. An Earth Defender vessel is one million kilometers behind us and closing."

"Navigation Command." The blue light flashed, and I smiled.

"What is their ETA?"

"At present speed, the craft will arrive in six hours, twenty-three minutes."

"What is the spec for the ship?"

"I don't have that information. I am a Navigation system."

I came close to earning an expletive fine but instead said "Information Command."

"Good afternoon, señor Hut." Information had a Mexican accent.

"The ship pursuing us. What's the spec for this vessel?"

"I do not know which vessel you need the specification for."

"Navigation Command. Link to Information Command," I hissed.

"Done, Hut."

The Information system emitted a series of blue flashes and then spoke.

"Ship is Defender, class B military craft. It has eight missile launchers and twenty heavy ballistic guns. Maximum troop capacity is 40 humans. The designation denotes a Space Marshal craft. There are likely 10-15 Marshals on board."

"Probable attack scenario?"

"They will hail us on the local holo channel and demand to board us."

"What will they do if we refuse?"

"Records show that in all previous encounters, the alleged perpetrators agreed to be boarded."

"Can they board if we do not offer them a space bridge?"

"No. Technically, they have no way to breach our ship without puncturing our hull. That would kill us all."

"What is the protocol for their alternative to boarding?"

"They will use their cannons to disable us and have another space tractor tow us to a landing site for arrest." I wouldn't say I liked the sound of this.

Six hours later, I received a holo-call from the Defender.

"Ahoy, Hut Mur. This is the Defender Worldview." The man in the hologram wore the uniform of a Space Marshal junior commander, as I had expected.

I stepped into the hologram. "Hello. To whom do I have the pleasure to be communicating?"

"I am Special Agent, Fop Grem. I recognize you, Mr. Mur, from your identifier."

"You're a long way from Earth, Special Agent."

"You must have known you couldn't outrun us. Why did you even attempt it?"

"Why would I want to outrun you? I don't even know what you want with us. Or are you just passing through?"

"Nice try but it won't work. I have a warrant for your arrest along with Ms. Flama Omm and someone called Skrog."

"What are the charges?"

"Attempted extortion."

"Extorting who?"

"You know that. World Energy Corporation."

"What if I told you that we did not attempt to extort anyone and we have a registered contract with World Energy? It states that they will pay for a metal we have in our cargo pods. They're trying to weasel out of the deal and have made you a partner in their crime."

"I don't know about that and frankly I don't care. I have warrants and will serve them. I'm to take you three into custody and return to Earth."

"How do you intend to do that?"

Fop Grem hesitated. "We'll board you."

"How? Unless we extend our space bridge to link with yours, you have no way to enter our vessel."

"I'm ordering you to extend your bridge."

I gave Grem my best smile. "You may order us to do so, but I'm refusing."

"I don't want to have to use force."

"What force do you have in mind?"

The Special Agent seemed hesitant. "We have missiles and ballistic guns."

"And you are prepared to use them to arrest someone for attempted extortion. You're prepared to risk killing all of us?"

"Hey, Hut. Be reasonable."

"I am being reasonable."

"You won't surrender to us?"

"No chance."

"I need to talk with my superior." He terminated the holo-call.

Fop Grem came back on the call a half hour later.

"Mr. Mur. If you do not allow us to board your ship and take you, and your crew, into custody, I'm authorized to fire on your ion fusion engines. I'll disable them and request a Rescue Tractor to tow you back to Earth where we'll process the arrest."

Flama was not in the hologram but sneered. "Tell him I'm not crew." Then she paused and gave me a loving smile. "Being crew is rather a nice thought, though."

My heart melted but I knew that I was facing a difficult situation, so my mind snapped back to the space marshal. I guessed that Special Agent Grem was not very experienced. The hologram showed him to be about twenty-five years of age. This might even be his first mission. "Special Agent, do you know what you are threatening? If you use ballistic cannons on my engines, it is likely to trigger a nuclear explosion killing all on my ship and scattering radioactive materials across space. It may even cause significant damage to your vessel. I can't believe you or your superiors would want that. And if you survived, you would be charged with murder when attempting to arrest people for a low-level felony." The hologram has precision optics, and I could read his expression. He was flustered and was wondering if his superior understood the risks. Perhaps, his boss didn't even care.

He spoke with hesitation. "I need to check. I'll reconnect the call later."

Another hour passed and then he resumed the holo-call. "My superior, on Earth is satisfied that we can fire a shot that will disable you without risk of an explosion. My crew has no experience with this approach but thinks it'll work."

I laughed out loud. "And you believe him. At the end of the day, it'll be you who'll take the fall if you make the wrong decision."

"I'll repeat my demands, Captain Mur. Extend your bridge and accept your arrest or we'll engage with you. You have five minutes to comply."

I terminated the call and looked at Flama and Skrog. "I bet that he'll muster up his courage and take the shot."

"Big problem, Cap."

Grem came back on a few minutes later. "Last chance, Mur. Open your sky bridge or we'll fire on you."

I had already discussed the options with Skrog and Flama and we had jointly decided that when it reached this point we would capitulate. I sighed.

A voice with a French accent interrupted us as Navigation delivered an alert: "Spacecraft approaching from the direction of Mars."

"About time …"

I spoke clearly. "Navigation Command. Identify the vessel." I thought I knew and crossed my fingers.

The system answered. "It is a modified Speeder. A Martian Combat craft."

"Special Agent Grem, I'm adding another party to our call." I dialed the approaching vessel, and the holo-call expanded to include a three-hundred-pound, four-foot-tall Martian dressed in a military uniform.

"I am General Smarg of Martian Central Forces. I here on combat craft by order of High President. Defender Worldview you threatening Martian citizen, Skrog. You have no right to do."

Grem showed his confusion and indecision. "This Skrog person is one of three for whom I have arrest warrants. He is a fugitive. Please stand down so we can continue with the arrest."

The general wobbled. "Not accept. We armed vessel and fight you. Operate under Accords 3685.35. You outside Earth space. You closer Mars. We in charge this location."

Skrog ordered the camera system to show a magnified view of the general's ship. It had light armaments and was usually used for policing work on the Mars settlement. The Defender outgunned it, and if it came to a battle, the Defender would win easily. However, such an engagement would create a huge intersystem political firestorm.

Grem gasped, paused the holo-call, and stepped out of the image.

I gestured my thanks to the general and he bubbled.

As we waited for Grem's response, a dialog was taking place between a senior general on Mars and the head of the Space Marshals service on Earth. I have added the transcript of this conversation below.

TRANSCRIPT - WSM-00675-31791
Mars Defense Forces HQ
Mars Colony
and
Space Marshals HQ
Miami

March 27, 2091/10:14 A.M.
Classification: Originally government

Holo-call

Senior General, Martian Colony: Director Lom, I give you greet.

Director Space Marshals Service: And greetings to you, High General Krome. How can I help you?

Senior General Martian Colony: There major problem in space near Mars.

Director Space Marshals Service: Go on.

Senior General Martian Colony: Your Defender ship attack Martian citizen. Must stop.

Director Space Marshals Service: I do have a craft in that area, but the marshals are on a police matter. We are arresting three people for extortion—nothing to bother Mars.

Senior General Martian Colony: Actually, one person you want arrest is Martian.

Director Space Marshals Service: I didn't know there was a Martian on board, but I have orders from World Justice to arrest these people. Warrants were prepared, and we are obliged to serve them.

Senior General Martian Colony: Martian High President has agreement your president. Martians move to Earth. Leave Mars. Press talk big about. Martian citizen, you arrest negotiated deal. Is hero. No arrest. If arrested, major political problem.

Director Space Marshals Service: I understand your concern, but these three people on the space tractor allegedly committed crimes. We'll arrest them, but the court system will determine whether they are guilty or not.

Senior General Martian Colony: High President command me to protect this ship. My general in field will fight your Defender. My president threatens go to media with story of attack. Racism against Martians. Maybe war if no backdown. You get blame.

Director Space Marshals Service: I see your point and I certainly don't want to create a major incident. Let me check with my president. Although we are an independent authority with no direct linkage and are not subject to political pressure, we do not want to start an intersystem conflict. I'll investigate it and get back to you.

We waited for Grem's response, and over an hour passed. Flama was on tenterhooks, expecting that at any minute, the Defender would fire on us.

She looked over at me. "What's going on? Did they accept General Smarg's ultimatum or not?"

"Smarg informed Skrog that the higher-ups are negotiating something."

"I wish they would get on with it. This uncertainty is killing me." Flama lapsed into silence as she seemed to be thinking about the term she had just used - "killing me".

A few minutes later, Grem came back on the call. "Hello. I have received new orders from my superior and will be leaving you now to return to Earth. It seems there was a miscommunication. I apologize for any inconvenience and wish you a good day. Is there anything else I can assist you with at present?"

After the Defender departed, General Smarg called me and chattered in his simplified English for a short time. Then he spoke with Skrog in his own language before ordering his Speeder to chart a course back to Mars. We were left alone in space.

Flama posed the question on all of our minds. "What do we do now? We haven't been arrested so we won't be ending up in a penal colony. But we don't have the money we were promised."

I answered her, "We have nine cargo pods loaded with Delt, which no one seems to need anymore. Our claim for the metal is recorded, and we can defend that in court. However, it has no commercial value, so our ownership doesn't matter. I'm sure that World Energy will refuse to pay, and they'll out lawyer us in the courts for a year or more."

Skrog looked at both of us - three eyes focused on each. "Go back Delta23? Dump Delt there?"

Chapter Eighteen

Meanwhile, a meeting was taking place in Greenland, on Earth, which would affect our future dramatically.

> **TRANSCRIPT - WPG-29965-62174**
> **World Power Grid (WPG) Research Division**
> **Nuuk, Greenland**
> **April 1, 2091/1:12 P.M.**
> **Classification: Originally marked Personal - recoded Business**

Scientist 1: Sir, I have terrible news.

Scientist 2: I don't see what that could be. We've recovered the payment made to Hut Mur and the Space Marshals are probably closing in on him as we speak. We don't need the Delt anymore and that has saved our parent corporation trillions of dollars. What could be so bad?

Scientist 1: I don't know how to phrase this. I can't see how to make it more positive.

Scientist 2: Oh, get on with it. I'm a busy man.

Scientist 1: We've been monitoring the reactivation of the Delt in the test batteries.

Scientist 2: And?

Scientist 1: Revitalization seems to be only temporary. It worked well but, after a week or two, the batteries in the test showed some deterioration. Then, they reverted to their fully depleted state.

Scientist 2: Good God, man. Re-charge them again. You probably got it wrong.

Scientist 1: We tried that and it didn't work. We tried several times. We attempted a lot of other approaches, but none worked."

Scientist 2: What's the answer? We must have an answer.

Scientist 1: We need the new Delt, after all.

TRANSCRIPT - WPG-29997-01401
World Power Grid (WPG) HQ
Nuuk, Greenland
April 2, 2091/1:12 P.M.
Classification: Originally marked Personal - recoded Business

Grid Executive: Fuck!

Voice recorder: NAME REDACTED is fined $100.

Grid Executive: You scientists are driving me crazy. First, you needed the new Delt, and then you didn't. Now we're back to needing it. When is this going to end?

Scientist 2: We thought we had it solved with the reenergizing process but that didn't work out. We need the fresh metal after all.

Grid Executive: The only supply of that is still with Hut Mur.

Scientist 2: Yes. Well, maybe. He probably still has it, but last time I checked he was heading toward Mars pursued by the Space Marshals. They should have caught up to him by now. But we told him that it had no value, so he may have dumped it. Or the Space Marshals may have attacked him and, accidentally, destroyed it.

Grid Executive: If you are religious, now is the time to pray that he didn't ditch it and the marshals didn't destroy it. This is just incompetence on your part. Even if he still has it, we can't follow through accusing him of extortion. The Delt would be tied up in court until the Grid implodes. We'll have to pay him the money. It's going to cost World Energy a fortune. That's even if he is prepared to deal.

Scientist 2: We can try.

Grid Executive: Our illustrious CEO is going to be really pissed with us. Especially with you."

TRANSCRIPT - WEC-56320-17931
World Energy Corporation (WEC)HQ
New York
and
World Power Grid (WPG) HQ
Nuuk, Greenland
April 3, 2091/1:12 P.M.
Classification: Originally marked Personal - recoded Business

Holo-call

Cal Rena: You're fired.

Grid Executive: Sir, it's not my fault.

Cal Rena: Well, whose fault is it? Not mine. I made the initial deal with Mur, and then you told me that we didn't need the Delt. You concocted the charge against him and lodged it with the Court under World Energy's name. Now you tell me that we do need the metal. You got that wrong, didn't you?

Grid Executive: Yes. But…

Cal Rena: I just had a call from the president, and he informed me that Mur enlisted the help of the Martians who interceded. The Space Marshals decided, not to start a war and stood down. Just as well. Do we know if Mur still has the Delt?

Grid Executive: I assume he has.

Cal Rena: I'm fed up with your assumptions.

On my tractor, we were out of danger but still debating what to do next. I grinned. "Well, we're not dead nor arrested but we're not rich anymore either."

Flama said, "So much for my negotiating skills. They were a waste of time, weren't they? My great achievement was for nothing." She broke out into laughter, a rare emotion for the woman.

I smiled at her. "I do believe that you just laughed at yourself."

"You're right. And without a TESVG course."

Skrog bubbled and said, "All safe. Close escape. Let's celebrate." He reached over and withdrew a bottle of gin and one of whiskey from the drink cabinet.

Flama eyed the Galactic-branded spirits and shook her head. "So much for being able to afford a better gin."

She poured herself one and added a little less tonic than normal, "But, I'm worried."

I looked at her. "What about this time?"

She swilled the drink down. "I'm starting to like Galactic. My taste buds must be totally destroyed."

I looked at her and my smile left me.

She interrupted my thoughts. "I can see what you're thinking Hut Mur."

I scowled.

"Since we don't have our trillions, you think that I'm going to dump you? You think I'll want you to take me back to an Earth shuttle."

I didn't answer her as I processed the effect it would have on me when she walked away.

I responded, "I can't blame you. You've been clear about what you want and need."

She let out a joyful laugh. "Not so fast, space cadet. You can't get rid of me that easily. You said you loved me and I told you that I loved you. You're stuck with me as we explore the universe in your tractor. Your generation 2, with upgrades, tractor. I like the idea of a Level A relationship, by the way." She curled up on the sofa next to me. "I've had a lot of time to think. This spaceship is cramped but I can live with that. Partnering with a space captain would be cool. That's if you'll have me. However, I would like to have the bedroom painted a different color and we need some scatter cushions."

I took her in my arms and kissed her. Skrog bubbled more than I have ever seen him do.

My heart was singing when a tone interrupted notifying us of a call on the holo-system and I checked the Caller ID.

I was surprised to see that it was Cal Rena.

"What does that low life want now?"

I motioned for us all to move to the Control Center, and I answered the call.

Cal Rena's image appeared, and he had a broad smile on his face which I knew he was faking. What new stunt are you about to pull? I wondered.

He started the call. "Hello Hut. My dear, boy. It's so great to chat again. I gather the Space Marshals have stopped their awful harassment of you. It was a terrible misunderstanding. An executive of mine acted without my authority and I've fired him."

My curiosity was running wild and Flama, from off-screen, whispered, "Ask him what he wants?" I glared at her.

I spoke confidently despite being mystified by the call. "Well, sir, it was a terrifying experience. Being chased by the marshals and then being informed that they were about to fire on us was harrowing. We have recordings of the entire incident, and I shall be sending them off to our attorney bot."

He nodded. "I understand completely. And I apologize. What can I say? Are you and your crew safe and sound?"

"Well, Mr. Rena, if it had not been for some Martian friends making a clear point to the marshals, we probably would have been space dust by now."

Rena shook his head. "Oh, Hut. That would have never happened. I'm sure."

Flama butted in. "You weren't here, Mr. Rena. The marshals said they were acting on an indictment triggered by World Energy."

The World Energy CEO was starting to become flustered. "That was a rogue executive from our Grid unit. As soon as I found out what was happening, I acted as rapidly as I could."

"Liar," said Flama from outside the holographic image.

I decided to take a blunt approach: "Tell me, sir. What do you want? I can't believe that you would call me to apologize."

Then he made everything clear.

"Mr. Mur. Do you still have the Delt?"

Chapter Nineteen

By the end of April 2091, we had returned to Earth orbit and offloaded the nine pods of Delt for its final passage to the planet. World Energy had paid us, and I checked that the money had been deposited into our accounts.

As I nodded the confirmation to Flama and Skrog, Flama asked the question that I had expected. "World Energy has the Delt and will start to swap out the depleted batteries. And we are rich. Even richer after the final negotiation with Rena. We can choose to live anywhere in the Solar System. What do you want to do, Hut?"

"Perhaps I just pay off the tractor, and we live on board." For an instant, she appeared to think I was serious, but my grin gave me away.

She kissed me. "No way, Jose. It's Earth for us. But not some big city. Somewhere private and beautiful. Somewhere, we can watch the stars and planets at night but not be in the solitude of space."

At the beginning of this book, I asked you, the reader, to guess where I would end up. The choices were:

5. In solitary confinement at a penal colony on Saturn.

6. On an island in the Caribbean.

7. In a spacecraft nearly three hundred million kilometers from Earth... being pursued by Space Marshals.

8. On an unpopulated piece of rock five hundred million kilometers from Earth. An asteroid called Delta23.

It was the second alternative - On an island in the Caribbean.

Did you get the answer right?

In June 2091, I purchased what was previously known as Saint-Barthelemy, more often referred to as St. Barts.

It had been French-owned since the 17th century, but in 2052, France, in a financial crisis, sold it to Clar Dass, a senior executive in Northern Hemisphere Banking and Investment Corporation. Ms. Dass was easily able to afford the cost having made a fortune shorting the French state and a few other countries in that same crisis.

Taking ownership of the Caribbean paradise, she generously paid the inhabitants to leave their homes and move to more temperate locations. With the sweltering temperatures from climate change, they were happy to do so, and many rented properties in Nova Scotia.

She installed an extensive, outdoor, air-conditioning system to combat the rising heat and consolidated the living arrangements into four large houses across the island where she entertained clients and friends.

As Ms. Dass aged and became increasingly busy with her global business activities, the executive and her family rarely traveled to the island and regarded it a folly. What seemed a good idea at the time she purchased it, had become an unused, expensive albatross for the banker.

Recently, when her fifth husband divorced her, and she needed funds to settle with him, she agreed to sell and I bought it for a high, but reasonable, price. The price included the 800% transaction tax levied on this "luxury" property. I half expected a "thank you" note from the World Council but was not surprised when I did not receive one. Oh well.

Before completing the purchase, I negotiated with Ms. Dass for weeks but being the richest man on planet Earth and sharing the island with Flama, the richest woman, the price didn't matter. However, I wanted to show Flama my ability to negotiate.

After we had closed on the property, Flama and I settled comfortably on the island in a Level A relationship. The bots had a field day with the prenuptial agreement.

We occupy three of the four houses that Dass built and have two private aircraft capable of worldwide travel and negotiating the short runway. The planes had tax rates of over 1,000%! After the restricted life on my space tractor, we both treasure the spaciousness of the island and our dwellings. All our lounge areas are twenty times the size of those on my tractor. Each villa has multiple swimming pools, but we have fun plunging into the turquoise sea of the Caribbean as well. I learned to swim for the first time. Flama liked our pools but reveled in the freedom of the beaches and the sea as well.

We commissioned four personal restaurants across the island each of which has a human master chef and a different cuisine. French, Italian, Asian, and Caribbean. Flama chooses the menus and, on a day-to-day basis, manages that part of our life. We use robo-driving electric sports vehicles to travel from our houses to the restaurants. The vehicles have manual alternative systems so, now and then, we take hands-on control which brings with it an amazing thrill that most Earthlings no longer experience. So far, we have, narrowly, avoided accidents.

Maintenance and service is provided by a bevy of robots.

The island is designated by the World Court as a separate country and we have a reasonable level of autonomy. One such aspect has been to ensure that the voice recorders installed by law, are not well-maintained and, frankly, are not operational.

We share the island with one other couple. The male is a four-foot, 300-lb. Martian, Skrog, who lives in the fourth house, a campus outside Gustavia, which had been the main town. He shares this with his new companion, Flomp, who is also a Martian.

After the World Council implemented the Martian Relocation resolution, the Martians started moving to their new home in central Mongolia, and Skrog was honored by his High Parliament. The High President himself made the award in a historic address broadcast across the Solar System. He spoke in his own language but then repeated the highlights in English. "Skrog. It is you persuade World Council ratify agreement relocate to Earth. We now leave temporary quarters on Mars. I bestow you honor of Hero of …"

Sorry, I still can't pronounce the planet's name.

In addition to his honor, my Martian friend became betrothed to his childhood sweetheart, the eldest daughter of the High President. She was 110 years old at the time of their relationship Level A nuptials and they expect their first child in four months.

Meanwhile, the Grid quietly swapped out all its batteries globally, and today, World Energy and the Grid operate smoothly. Few on Earth know just how close the planet's population was to a major catastrophe. The press has been encouraged to call stories about the threat a "fake media scare."

The World Council asked me not to publish this account but since you are reading it, you will know that I declined their request. The Public Relations office has insisted that I categorize it as "fiction".

However, the world's highest elected officials suffered from revelations about their secret deal.

You may remember that on March 17, Earth's president and vice president discussed their questionable relationship with World Energy and expected the recording of their meeting to be deleted. The voice recorder system overrode this and the transcript was later discovered and leaked to the media. The story ran for several weeks. Both men resigned in disgrace and new politicians were elected to their roles. Voting was still compulsory and all Earth citizens recorded their preferences remotely using their implanted chips for identification. People who did not vote were fined and the system ensured that each citizen voted only once. My current assessment of the replacements to the Presidential offices is that they do not appear to be less corrupt than the two they replaced.

Cal Rena, the Chief Executive of World Energy, was also implicated, and to avoid a lengthy jail sentence, he resigned from his lucrative employment. He awarded himself a significant retirement stipend, but the shareholders turned this down. He left with heavy personal debt and little stock holding or monetary credit. I cannot say that I feel sorry for him although he had agreed to Flama's revised price for the Delt adding billions of dollars to what World Energy paid us. I have lost track of the man but cannot help thinking our paths will cross sometime.

Anyway, I must end my writing now. Flama and I are going out on our new jet boat. The tax on this was 950%! We have our air-conditioned jackets with us and are going fishing. Despite the warming of the Caribbean, as with most other seas and oceans, the fish have seemed to adapt. Some have left for cooler waters, but others have embraced the changed environment and there are some huge Wahoo out there.

Flama wore a sporty green bikini, and, at her bidding, I dressed in a matching swimsuit that seemed a little too sparse. We walked down to the dock, where Skog and Flomp were to join us. While waiting for them, Flama came over and threw her arms around me, smothering me in kisses.

"Oh, Hut. I love you more every day. And your new swimsuit is terrific—great color!"

I groaned and thought about returning to the house and changing. Oh well.

She looked at me and I knew she had read my mind. Letting out a loud laugh, she added. "We must think up a suitable name for the new boat."

She watched closely as I groaned again.

Over the months since we finalized the deal with World Energy, we had become even closer than before, and we both knew that we were wholly in love with each other. It is not just sex. Well, probably, it is not just sex.

The four of us boarded the fifty-meter vessel. It is sleek and made from laminated titanium, mined on another asteroid in the Belt, with stainless steel accents. It is dark blue, which contrasts well with the turquoise of the sea. It reminded me of the Speeder that Kul had used when he flew up to Jupiter to meet us.

I was wearing a captain's cap denoting my role on the craft and I stood upright on the control deck. I regarded the array of instruments before me including an old-fashioned steering wheel although I knew the system was wholly voice-operated. My three companions quietly waited for me to start the engines.

Smiling at them, I spoke with confidence. "Boat Command".

The blue light did not flash.

The End

A Note from the Author - Worldbuilding

Delta23 is set in the year 2091 – sixty-seven years from today – and to provide a backdrop to the story, I needed to create, what is known as worldbuilding. This is my invention of what life will be like in that futuristic time. It provided an anchor for how the plot plays out and needs to be a believable and defensible scenario. It reflects the changes that might be expected over the next third century, which some people will view positively and others not. I built these into a chronology and crafted my story around them.

The main themes:

- A third World War, in 2047, pushed mankind to recognize and accept, its potential for extinction.

- An alien force from a doomed planet outside the Solar System that populated Mars, wished to move to Earth and pressured the world government to abandon warfare. This caused the world to implement changes including disbanding all, in-country, armed forces.

- After the War, most economic activities were centralized at a world/global level, including:

    - A global government - the World Council

    - Standard laws across all countries

    - A World Court comprising AI-based judgments for simple cases and first-level appeals. A High Court of Final Appeal has fifteen human judges with no political affiliation elected by their peers for limited terms

    - A common language worldwide – English

    - A standard global currency – the World dollar

    - A worldwide, solar and wind, sustainable power grid that provides electricity

    - Wholly digital financial transactions. Cash is no longer used or accepted.

    - Replacement of income tax by a worldwide transaction tax (a.k.a. sales tax) using variable tax rates depending on what is being purchased. - low rate for commodities, very high rate for luxury goods. This is administered by AI using computer systems established to support a cashless society. Rates are adjusted to provide balanced funding for government programs

- Chips are implanted at birth for identification, financial transactions, licenses, voting, and medical records.

- A remote working model is prevalent and driven by continuing strains of COVID.

  o An at-home, AI-based teaching platform with children from age 3 who are instructed according to their capabilities, interests, and learning style by personalized instruction. Training for practical skills, education, and social aspects are taught and then followed by a recommendation on the child's vocation. Job placement follows. Graduation and employment start at eighteen, but smarter students, learning more advanced subjects, may stay in class through their early thirties.

- Home and vehicle ownership has shifted to lifetime rental of dwellings, and robo-taxis have replaced personal vehicles.

- Major changes, both medical and cultural, have been introduced, and over time, adopted, to provide surrogate birth using artificial wombs, lifetime pregnancy protection, and the elimination of women's mensural cycles and menopause. Testing for likely deceases and vaccination are implemented before birth.

- All verbal conversations are automatically recorded. Transcripts for business and governmental conversations are available through the World Freedom of Information Act but personal calls are held securely and can be accessed only by the participants in the conversation.

I do not endorse any of the themes in building this world. Some may seem too extreme, and others seem too slow a transition based on the speed at which change has occurred in recent history.

The worldbuilding is set sixty-seven years in the future and looking back sixty-seven years, to the year 1957, we find a world where:

- Just twenty computers (mainframes) were installed worldwide mainly in U.S. Government agencies.

- 75% of U.S. households had telephones, but they were black, heavy, wired devices with rotary dials, used principally for emergencies.

- Television was gaining in popularity on black-and-white sets tuned to 2-3 channels with mainly live programming. Even in the United States, only 20% of households owned a set.

- Commercial airflights used propellor-driven aircraft rather than jets which came later. A flight from New York to London took 15 hours. An ocean-going liner was preferred.

We have come a long way since then and, in 2091, our descendants will determine how accurate my worldbuilding has been.

About the Author:

Harry Bunn is known for his spy thriller series, Purple Frog and a nonfiction book on Customer Experience strategies for B2B companies. He has now embraced a new genre with Delta23 – adventure/romance set in the future.

Harry has traveled to over fifty countries worldwide, and has resided in Sydney, Australia; London, England; and Princeton, NJ. He founded an international marketing consulting firm focused on the technology sector, managed it for thirty years, and is now retired in St. Croix in the U.S. Virgin Islands, where he lives with his wife, Jackie. They have two sons, James and Nicholas.

Contact him at harrybunnauthor@gmail.com.

The Purple Frog Books

Purple Frog (Book 1)

Jason Overly, a technology billionaire, funds a daring rogue operation devoted to world peace. This international team employs unorthodox methods, including hacking, blackmail, extortion, and occasionally, murder. The group has been given the name Purple Frog after a little-known frog that spends most of its time underground, out of sight, emerging only for two weeks each year. Keeping below the radar is key to Purple Frog's success, but a plot to assassinate the new president of the European Union calls for more direct action and the risk of discovery.

MetalWorks (Book 2)

Frederik Verwoerd is successful and rich but wants more. He desires to become a major player on the world stage and decides that his South African armament company, MetalWorks, will develop a new weapon of mass destruction, which he will sell to the highest bidder. The weapon is neither nuclear, chemical, nor biological, but can destroy an army of five thousand tanks in the field, or even a major city. To demonstrate its power, he targets a well-protected symbol of the United States and will telecast its destruction live.

It falls to Purple Frog, a private and clandestine organization, to stop him. To do so, Purple Frog must reveal its existence to the CIA. However, the Russian president has already threatened to locate and punish the organization.

Brotherhood of the Skull (Book 3)

Outside Washington, DC, one million armed white supremacists have assembled to march on the capital and seize power. They are led by Gideon Page, a charismatic but ruthless white supremacist, and Jonathan Greer, a televangelist. They have a symbol for their insurrection: an ancient skull previously owned by Adolf Hitler. A rogue U.S. senator, Jeffrey Kendall, has teamed up with them and expects to become the new president of the United States after the Brotherhood of the Skull overthrows the present elected government.

Law enforcement is hamstrung by legalities and political correctness, but the clandestine Purple Frog organization has no such limitations and moves to thwart this attack on American democracy.

Citadel of Yakutsk (Book 4)

"The Citadel is the real threat." The dying words of the CIA Chief of Station in Moscow are cryptic, but no one knows what his message means. Yakutsk is a remote city in Siberia. It boasts the coldest weather of any city on the planet and is home to a clandestine facility in subterranean caves deep beneath the conurbation. This secret metropolis is the headquarters of Alexi Rackov, a Russian general who has developed a plan to expand Russian territory by invading eight countries and bringing eighty-eight million European citizens under Russian hegemony. While there are rumors about such a site, these only identify its name: the Citadel. Its location and mission are known only to Rackov and Dobry Petrovski, the Russian president.

In the United States, Purple Frog is a secret organization established by Jason Overly, a tech billionaire, with the mission to foster world peace. Though Purple Frog parallels the CIA and MI6, it operates outside the rules and political correctness of these intelligence organizations. It will face its greatest challenge as its small team strives to prevent the annexation of these Eastern European countries.

Flag Eight (Book 5)

A new president in Venezuela, Mateo Videgain, is facing a multitude of problems, including a collapsed economy. He regards the United States as a major reason for this and his main enemy, deciding on a bold plan to consolidate his place in history.

Just 520 miles to the north is the U.S. territory of St. Croix, and Videgain decides to invade and occupy the island.

All hell breaks loose as, with help from Russia, his helicopters, warships, and troops attack. When the locals fight back against his vastly superior forces, the battle is short and the Venezuelans take control.

Few countries have been ruled by seven different nations, but over the five hundred and twenty-eight years since Christopher Columbus discovered St. Croix, it has been a territory of Spain, France, the Netherlands, England, the Knights of Malta, Denmark, and most recently, the U.S. In total, seven flags have flown over the island. The Venezuelan president raises his flag over the territory—flag eight.

He has not, however, factored in that Jason Overly, who has a home on the island, is also the head of a clandestine intelligence operation called Purple Frog, which will do whatever is necessary to stop the Venezuelan president's plans.

To Venice with Love (Book 6)

Alan Harlan and his new wife, Jess, embark on their honeymoon to a Greek island, but they encounter an old enemy and a Saudi prince who have deployed a bioweapon on an ecologically advanced super yacht. Alan and Jess find themselves on the vessel's maiden voyage from Athens to Venice, discover the plot, and need to identify which of the passengers or crew will be responsible for triggering the device on their arrival in Venice.

Alan is head of operations for Purple Frog, a clandestine organization that mirrors the CIA and MI6 but with fewer constraints. He brings many of Purple Frog's resources into play as they battle the forces striving to destroy this romantic Italian city's population and one million visiting tourists.

Delete Code (Book 7)

Mike Young, a computer hacker, develops a set of malware that can delete every file and every piece of software from any computer that he targets. Initially, he sees this as an approach to extort money, but others see it as a powerful weapon of destruction. After successful demonstrations of the code's power, a major enemy of the United States develops a plan to use it to further its goal of world domination. The cybersecurity forces in government and the corporate world find themselves unable to counter the threat, so it falls to the hackers and field operations staff of Purple Frog to isolate and remove the danger.

Brisa's Grief (Book 8)

The head of a drug cartel, a billionaire, a spy's wife, and a killer experience grief and resolve it in different ways.

A DEA team raids the headquarters of a South American drug cartel, but things don't go as planned and the daughter of the cartel chief seeks revenge on the United States. She develops a new narcotic which she plans to release, killing several million Americans.

With political tensions running high, the U.S. governmental agencies are unable to act, and the task of preventing the disaster falls to Purple Frog, a clandestine organization devoted to world peace but without the constraints of conventional intelligence organizations.

Assault and Battery (Book 9)

November Swan is the third richest person in the world, but his portfolio of companies is turning sour. To tackle this threat, he decides to go "all in" acquiring a startup company that is developing next-generation, solid-state batteries for electric vehicles.

His plan requires access to rare earth components which are needed for large-scale manufacturing. These are located only in China.

Having always skirted the law and regulations, Swan pushes into more criminal acts to achieve his objectives, including a deal with China that puts the U.S. economy and its security in peril.

The Purple Frog team is tasked with stopping him.

Final Bow (Book 10)

In the face of an unstoppable force, the only option left is to fight back.

In Final Bow, the world hangs in the balance as an alliance of China, Russia, North Korea, and Iran develops an offensive they call "Global Strike." With the future of the Western world at stake, the clandestine spy team at Purple Frog must decide whether to use their own bold and risky plan for world peace, accepting its ethical and practical risks.

With the stakes so high, the tension builds as each move brings them closer to the ultimate showdown and the death of one of Purple Frog's leadership team becomes a final bow.

Non-Fiction

Customer Experience: It's not that easy.

Customer Experience Programs for B2B Companies

Customer Experience programs are gaining momentum in small and large companies, but most have been designed for the Business-to-consumer (B2C) model. When the approaches that work for B2C are applied in the Business-to-business (B2B) world, they fail.

Based on 27 years of experience consulting to major, global B2B companies, including IBM, Hewlett-Packard, Microsoft, Dell, VMware, EMC, Samsung, AT&T, Verizon, BT, Telefonica, Honeywell, Motorola, Accenture, Nokia, Siemens, Fujitsu, and Xerox, Harry Bunn sets out practical approaches for the B2B world. This book shows how Customer Experience can be built into the culture, the strategies, and the actions of companies, together with the mechanics required to "get it right". It shows how current customer satisfaction programs can be transformed into Customer Experience programs providing companies with sustainable, competitive differentiation.

Printed in Great Britain
by Amazon